Love Jo...

"I am prepared to follow you to Heaven or Hell. I pledge my allegiance."

He looked at Clova for a long moment, then Tarquil, the Laird of Cowan, went down on one knee, and taking her hand, kissed it.

Clova knew it was the age-old obeisance given to the Chieftain of a Clan, but she could not help tightening her fingers on his.

He rose to his feet, and now he seemed to tower above her.

"If you need me," he said, "send for me, and I will come to you. But because I value my life, I prefer that it should be in the daytime."

"Are you really...suggesting that my people might kill you?" Clova looked up into his dark eyes.

"There is certainly one amongst them who would not hesitate to do so..."

A Camfield Novel of Love
by Barbara Cartland

"Barbara Cartland's novels are all distinguished by their intelligence, good sense, and good nature..."
—ROMANTIC TIMES

"Who could give better advice on how to keep your romance going strong than the world's most famous romance novelist, Barbara Cartland?"
—THE STAR

Camfield Place,
Hatfield
Hertfordshire,
England

Dearest Reader,

Camfield Novels of Love mark a very exciting era of my books with Jove. They have already published nearly two hundred of my titles since they became my first publisher in America, and now all my original paperback romances in the future will be published exclusively by them.

As you already know, Camfield Place in Hertfordshire is my home, which originally existed in 1275, but was rebuilt in 1867 by the grandfather of Beatrix Potter.

It was here in this lovely house, with the best view in the county, that she wrote *The Tale of Peter Rabbit*. Mr. McGregor's garden is exactly as she described it. The door in the wall that the fat little rabbit could not squeeze underneath and the goldfish pool where the white cat sat twitching its tail are still there.

I had Camfield Place blessed when I came here in 1950 and was so happy with my husband until he died, and now with my children and grandchildren, I know the atmosphere is filled with love and we have all been very lucky.

It is easy here to write of love and I know you will enjoy the Camfield Novels of Love. Their plots are definitely exciting and the covers very romantic. They come to you, like all my books, with love.

Bless you,

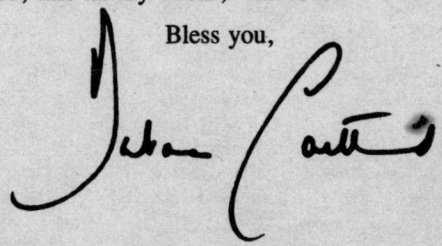

CAMFIELD NOVELS OF LOVE
by Barbara Cartland

- THE POOR GOVERNESS
- WINGED VICTORY
- LUCKY IN LOVE
- LOVE AND THE MARQUIS
- A MIRACLE IN MUSIC
- LIGHT OF THE GODS
- BRIDE TO A BRIGAND
- LOVE COMES WEST
- A WITCH'S SPELL
- SECRETS
- THE STORMS OF LOVE
- MOONLIGHT ON THE SPHINX
- WHITE LILAC
- REVENGE OF THE HEART
- THE ISLAND OF LOVE
- THERESA AND A TIGER
- LOVE IS HEAVEN
- MIRACLE FOR A MADONNA
- A VERY UNUSUAL WIFE
- THE PERIL AND THE PRINCE
- ALONE AND AFRAID
- TEMPTATION OF A TEACHER
- ROYAL PUNISHMENT
- THE DEVILISH DECEPTION
- PARADISE FOUND
- LOVE IS A GAMBLE
- A VICTORY FOR LOVE
- LOOK WITH LOVE
- NEVER FORGET LOVE
- HELGA IN HIDING
- SAFE AT LAST
- HAUNTED
- CROWNED WITH LOVE
- ESCAPE
- THE DEVIL DEFEATED
- THE SECRET OF THE MOSQUE
- A DREAM IN SPAIN
- THE LOVE TRAP
- LISTEN TO LOVE
- THE GOLDEN CAGE
- LOVE CASTS OUT FEAR
- A WORLD OF LOVE
- DANCING ON A RAINBOW
- LOVE JOINS THE CLANS

Other books by Barbara Cartland

- THE ADVENTURER
- AGAIN THIS RAPTURE
- BARBARA CARTLAND'S BOOK OF BEAUTY AND HEALTH
- BLUE HEATHER
- BROKEN BARRIERS
- THE CAPTIVE HEART
- THE COIN OF LOVE
- THE COMPLACENT WIFE
- COUNT THE STARS
- DESIRE OF THE HEART
- DESPERATE DEFIANCE
- THE DREAM WITHIN
- ELIZABETHAN LOVER
- THE ENCHANTING EVIL
- ESCAPE FROM PASSION
- FOR ALL ETERNITY
- A GOLDEN GONDOLA
- A HAZARD OF HEARTS
- A HEART IS BROKEN
- THE HIDDEN HEART
- THE HORIZONS OF LOVE
- IN THE ARMS OF LOVE
- THE IRRESISTIBLE BUCK
- THE KISS OF PARIS
- THE KISS OF THE DEVIL
- A KISS OF SILK
- THE KNAVE OF HEARTS
- THE LEAPING FLAME
- A LIGHT TO THE HEART
- LIGHTS OF LOVE
- THE LITTLE PRETENDER
- LOST ENCHANTMENT
- LOVE AT FORTY
- LOVE FORBIDDEN
- LOVE IN HIDING
- LOVE IS THE ENEMY
- LOVE ME FOREVER
- LOVE TO THE RESCUE
- LOVE UNDER FIRE
- THE MAGIC OF HONEY
- METTERNICH THE PASSIONATE DIPLOMAT
- MONEY, MAGIC AND MARRIAGE
- NO HEART IS FREE
- THE ODIOUS DUKE
- OPEN WINGS
- A RAINBOW TO HEAVEN
- THE RELUCTANT BRIDE
- THE SCANDALOUS LIFE OF KING CAROL
- THE SECRET FEAR
- THE SMUGGLED HEART
- A SONG OF LOVE
- STARS IN MY HEART
- STOLEN HALO
- SWEET ENCHANTRESS
- SWEET PUNISHMENT
- THEFT OF A HEART
- THE THIEF OF LOVE
- THIS TIME IT'S LOVE
- TOUCH A STAR
- TOWARDS THE STARS
- THE UNKNOWN HEART
- WE DANCED ALL NIGHT
- THE WINGS OF ECSTASY
- THE WINGS OF LOVE
- WINGS ON MY HEART
- WOMAN, THE ENIGMA

A NEW CAMFIELD NOVEL OF LOVE BY

BARBARA CARTLAND

Love Joins the Clans

A JOVE BOOK

LOVE JOINS THE CLANS

A Jove Book/published by arrangement with
the author

PRINTING HISTORY
Jove edition/April 1987

All rights reserved.
Copyright © 1987 by Barbara Cartland.
Cover art copyright © 1987 by Barcart Publications (N.A.) N.V.
This book may not be reproduced in whole or in part,
by mimeograph or any other means, without permission.
For information address: The Berkley Publishing Group,
200 Madison Avenue, New York, NY 10016.

ISBN: 0-515-08933-8

Jove Books are published by The Berkley Publishing Group,
200 Madison Avenue, New York, NY 10016.
The words "A JOVE BOOK" and the "J" with sunburst
are trademarks belonging to Jove Publications, Inc.

PRINTED IN THE UNITED STATES OF AMERICA

Author's Note

The feuds between the Clans are a great part of the history of Scotland. The last great Clan battle was fought between the MacDonalds and the Mackintoshes at Mulroy in 1688, but violent quarrels and braeside murders survived, and the old way of life in the Highlands was largely unchanged.

The Chief was still the father of the Clan, and possessed the terrible powers of his ancestors. There was no alternative to his protection and no appeal against his authority.

In that century, a Clanranald Chief would punish a thief by tying her hair to the seaweed on his coast, leaving her to drown in the Atlantic tide.

In the Eighteenth Century the English, having conquered the Scots, realised the supreme and unequalled fighting ability of the men from the Highlands. The raising of the Highland Regiments was instrumental in the creation of an Imperial Britain.

One of the first Regiments mustered by Simon Fraser of Lovat, Chief of the name, contained men who had fought at Culloden while some of them died with James Wolfe on the Heights of Abraham.

During the next fifty years the Crown drained the Highlands for twenty-seven line Regiments and nineteen Battalions of fencibles.

In the French wars at the turn of the century, the Highlanders supplied the British Army with the equivalent of seven or eight infantry divisions.

They were a unique and splendid Corps, united by a courage and loyalty unsurpassed by any other Regiment.

chapter one

1885

As the train carried her across England, Clova sat beside the window, thinking that what was happening could not be true.

It seemed incredible that only a few weeks ago she was in despair, fearing her mother would die of starvation before she did from the wasting disease the doctors had diagnosed.

Then she herself would either have to face the cold waters of the Seine, or surrender to the evils that were all too prevalent in Paris.

As the train moved swiftly through the countryside she realised that she had forgotten how green England had looked the first time she saw it, and wondered if Scotland would perhaps be more familiar.

She had been seven when her mother, the beautiful, laughing Charlotte McBlane, had run away with Lionel Arkwright, who had come to Scotland year after year to shoot the grouse on her grandfather's moors.

Even as a child, Clova had thought Lionel Arkwright was a charming man, gay and witty, very different from her father, who always appeared to be serious and disapproving.

Looking back now to when she was very young, Clova knew she had always been afraid of him.

Perhaps if she had been older she would have known it was merely his Scottish "dourness" that had made him seem frightening.

Her mother, she could understand, had found him dull.

It had been a brilliant match for the daughter of an unimportant retired English Colonel to marry the younger son of the Marquess of Strathblane.

But Lord Alister McBlane had been fascinated, then captivated by the eighteen-year-old Charlotte Burton, who was always called "Lottie."

As soon as Lottie looked at him with her huge blue eyes, he had known at once she was very different from the girls he knew in Scotland.

Lord Alister had been a guest of the Lord Lieutenant of Yorkshire for the Doncaster Races.

Lottie, who had been invited to the Balls that were given to entertain the race-goers from the South, had undoubtedly stood out even though the other women were far more important socially than she was.

Her figure was like thistledown, and her laughing eyes and golden hair made her the focus of attention from the moment she walked into any room.

Lord Alister was not the only man to be "bowled

over" by Lottie, but he was undoubtedly the most important.

When the races ended, he engineered quite blatantly an invitation to stay with Colonel Burton on the pretext that he wanted to see the rather indifferent horses he kept on the small estate which encircled the house in which he lived.

Mrs. Burton had been in a flutter.

"How could you possibly ask anyone so important," she enquired of her husband, "when you know the servants are hopeless, and I cannot get a decent cook?"

"I do not think His Lordship will be so much concerned about the food," Colonel Burton said dryly.

He already realised from Lord Alister's behaviour at the three Balls they had attended that Lottie was the inducement for his inviting himself to stay.

More than once Lottie was to be swept off her feet by the men who came into her life.

In an incredibly short time, almost indecently so, it was said in the countryside, Lottie was travelling to Scotland to live in the ugly, rather uncomfortable house on the Marquess's estate, which was considered quite good enough for a younger son.

Lord Alister did not complain.

He was used, Lottie found, to putting up with the crumbs that fell from the rich man's table—in his case, that of his father and of his elder brother, who was the heir to the Marquessate.

He accepted it, while later Lottie was to rage against the injustice of the relatively small allowance he received, the inferior horses he had to ride, and the uncouth, untrained servants who were all they could afford.

But looking back, which was difficult because she had been so young at the time, Clova thought that Lottie had been happy, or at least more or less content, until the Honourable Lionel Artwright came to stay with the Marquess.

Lottie was always prepared to accept any man who was available, unless there was one better to be ensnared.

It was difficult now for Clova to remember when she was first aware of Lionel Arkwright.

There were always quite a number of gentlemen staying with her grandfather in the shooting season.

Invariably they soon found their way into her mother's house, because whatever their age, Lottie drew them like a magnet.

By the time she was seven Clova was used to gentlemen who smelt of tweeds and expensive cigars putting their arms around her and saying:

"She is going to be as pretty as you, or very nearly, when she is grown up!"

Her mother always laughed and replied:

"You must not turn the child's head with your compliments!"

The invariable answer was:

"I wonder if it would be possible to turn yours?"

When they spoke to her mother in the voice that was somehow deeper than usual and had a caressing note in it, Clova would watch her mother look at them from under her eye-lashes.

She smiled in a way which appeared to have something shy about it, and yet was incredibly fascinating.

Clova realised that when there were gentlemen present her mother seemed to blossom and look more

4

beautiful than she did when she was alone with her father.

Then there were often long meals when he would hardly speak, and her mother would say impatiently:

"Are you listening to me, Alister?"

"Yes, dear, of course."

"What am I to do about Clova's pony? She is really too old for it and at her age she needs something larger and more spirited."

"I will see what I can do."

Clova knew from experience that this always meant her father could not afford it, or else he would forget once he had left the Dining-Room what her mother had been talking about.

He was immersed most of the time in breeding from the mares he bought in the South, but which did not always flourish in the cold bleakness of the North.

Yet he had persisted in trying to produce outstanding foals simply because, Clova decided now, there was little else for him to do.

His father, the Chieftain of the McBlanes, would not allow him to play any part in the running of the estate.

What the Marquess did not do himself, which was a great deal, was entrusted to Rory, his elder son, whom he obviously adored, while Alister bored him.

The two brothers had very little in common, and while Rory resembled his father, Clova had always believed that Alister took after his mother, who had died soon after his birth.

By all accounts, confirmed by her portrait, she had been a plain woman, but had brought with her a sizable dowry and belonged to a Clan that was favoured by the McBlanes.

It was Lottie who had opened her daughter's eyes years later as to the truth about their situation in Scotland.

"They despised poor Alister for having married a *Sassenach*, and one moreover with no money," she said. "Of course, as he had made his bed, he had to lie on it, and if it was hard and uncomfortable, those unyielding Scots were determined it was what he deserved for having been such a fool as to marry me!"

"But he loved you, Mama."

"Of course he loved me," Lottie replied, "as much as he was capable of loving anyone. He was not a very emotional man, and I have often wondered what he really felt when I ran away."

It was impossible for Clova to enlighten her because when her mother ran off with Lionel Arkwright, she had gone with them.

"I am not going to leave my baby behind me," Lottie had said in a burst of sentimentality, besides the fact that Clova was seven. "She is so pretty and so much like me that I know the McBlanes would make her suffer for my sins, and that I could not bear."

But Lottie herself had suffered for them.

At first everything had been wonderful. Lionel Arkwright was rich and he took them to Paris, where they had a delightful house just off the fashionable Champs-Élysées.

Lionel had a great many friends in the gayest Capital in Europe, and if most of their wives refused to meet a woman who was "living in sin," having dared to flout the conventions by running away from her husband, their husbands were only too eager to fête Lottie and to flirt with her.

Lionel Arkwright bought her clothes that were more expensive and certainly more beautiful than anything she had ever imagined, which made her look even more alluring than she was already.

When glittering with jewels she said goodnight to Clova, the small girl used to think her mother looked like a Fairy Queen in the picture-books that her Governess read to her.

If her mother found Paris entrancing, she did, too, and she realised for the first time that beauty could tug at her heart with a feeling which was wonderful, yet almost a pain.

The fountains playing in the Place de la Concorde, the chestnuts bursting into bloom in the Champs-Élysées, the Seine moving silver and slow under the bridges, all seemed to speak to her more eloquently than could any words.

She also enjoyed her lessons, finding they opened up new horizons she had never known existed with her Scots Nanny who had taught her first her alphabet, her arithmetic, and her prayers.

When she was ten disaster struck!

Lionel Arkwright's father died and he came into the title, inheriting an ancestral home and a large estate which was waiting for him in England.

Although he promised to return, Lottie knew this was the end.

Behaving like a gentleman, which he undoubtedly was, he settled on her quite a considerable amount of money.

Unfortunately, not content with living in Paris,

Lionel had taken her every Spring to Monte Carlo.

It was fashionable to be there and all their friends seemed to move with them, as did all the most famous actresses and the *demi-mondaines* whose hats were covered with osprey feathers and their necks with long strings of pearls.

The latter were as important a feature of the much-decried Capital of Monaco as the illustrious social figures who crowded into the small Principality, where the main attraction was of course the Casino.

Lottie found the roulette and the baccarat tables irresistible, and the first year after Lionel left her was not difficult.

There were always men whom she had known in Paris who were only too willing to pay her losses and allow her to keep her winnings and theirs also.

When the season was over and they returned to Paris to the house in which she had lived with Lionel Arkwright, Lottie found that he had sold it.

He had put some of the money obtained from the sale into the Bank in her name, but as Clova thought sadly, it was not the same as having a home, which the house had always been to her.

Now she learnt there were places where one could gamble in Paris also, and Lottie continued to dress in the same way she had when Lionel Arkwright had been with her.

Slowly and inevitably things became more and more difficult.

"I am afraid we shall have to move, darling," her mother would say.

It was a statement Clova had heard before.

"Oh, not again, Mama!"

"It is ridiculous how much we are paying for this apartment, and it is not worth it! It is dark and uncomfortable, and the bedrooms are too close together."

Clova knew that this was important, because when her mother came back late at night, she would wake up and hear her talking to a man who spoke in the same deep-voiced velvet tones that she had heard before.

Then suddenly they were rich again.

They would move into far more pleasant surroundings, and there would be another man whom she would be told to address as "Uncle."

In the years to come, "Uncles" were to follow each other in quick succession.

There was "Uncle François," who was, of course, French, and "Uncle Leon," who was a Banker.

"Uncle Antonio" had lasted only a short time before he returned to Rome, and then there was a succession of "Uncle" this and "Uncle" that, until she found it hard to remember them.

One thing was becoming obvious—her "Uncles" were growing older, and so was her mother.

Lottie was still lovely, but there were lines under her eyes that had not been there before, and she often seemed tired and listless, not only in the morning, but during the day as well.

"I am sure, Mama, you need a tonic," Clova would say.

"What I need is money!" her mother unwillingly retorted.

But because Clova was really worried, she had, a

year ago, insisted that her mother saw a really good doctor, a Specialist, as he was called.

He had examined Lottie and then while she was dressing he came into the room where Clova was waiting alone.

"I want to talk to you, *Mademoiselle*," he said, "and you must be very brave."

Clova's eyes widened.

"About Mama?"

"Yes, about your mother."

"What is it?"

She found it difficult to ask the question.

"I am afraid your mother has what is known as 'the Wasting Disease'—Tuberculosis is the medical name for it."

Clova had drawn in her breath.

"What . . . can we . . . do?"

"Very little, I am afraid. There is no known cure. You could take her to a Sanatorium in Switzerland, but I am afraid it would do very little good, and I feel sure she would dislike it."

"She would hate it!"

"Then may I suggest that you keep her as happy as possible, make her rest and eat properly."

He paused, then looked at Clova's white face and said:

"I am sorry to have to tell you this. But I understand your mother has no husband and no one else to look after her but you."

Clova had straightened her shoulders.

"I will manage," she said.

"I will come again at once if she suffers any real pain," the Specialist said, "but she may go on as she is now, just feeling tired, and needing a lot of love and understanding."

"I will do my best," Clova promised. "Have you told Mama the truth?"

The Specialist shook his head.

"I find it wiser in these cases not to let the patient have any idea of how serious her condition is."

Clova was sure that was wise where her mother was concerned, and when they left, Lottie had said to her:

"I call that a waste of money! He did not give me anything to make me feel more energetic. I will treat myself. It will be far easier!"

There was nothing Clova could do to stop her.

She was still lovely, though like all people with the "Wasting Disease" she was very thin.

Her thinness, however, seemed to accentuate the lissom fragility which had always been one of her attractions.

When she was amused by some man who was paying her a compliment, there would be a bright spot of colour in her cheeks, her eyes would shine, and she would look far younger than she really was and very lovely.

It was only the next morning that she was grey-faced and so tired that every movement was an enormous effort.

Clova did everything she could, but she had found a year or so previously, to her horror, that Lottie had gambled away nearly all the money that Lionel Arkwright had left her in the Bank.

Of course it had been augmented from time to time by other admirers, but inevitably the main capital dwindled month by month, year by year.

There were always men eager to take Lottie out to dinner, to give her champagne, to pay in other ways for their amusement.

But they were not prepared to pay the rent, as Lionel Arkwright had done, or provide for somebody else's child.

Soon there were no more Governesses, no more servants, and, as far as Clova was concerned, very little amusement.

By the time she had cleaned their apartment, helped her mother dress, washed and mended everything they wore, there was little time even to read a book.

"I think I will just go to the Hotel Meurice or the Crillon to see if there is anybody staying there I know," Lottie had said when she was dressed.

This meant she was hoping she would find an old friend, or perhaps a new one, who would buy her glasses of champagne and, if she were lucky, take her out to dinner, bringing her home in the early hours of the morning.

Sometimes a strange man would stay in their apartment overnight, and Clova would cook breakfast for the two of them and, on her mother's instructions, keep out of sight.

"I do not want anybody to see you, darling, and realise how poor we are, and how we have no servants," Lottie would explain.

Clova could understand this, and it had been enough to know that her mother was happy and laughing, as if she had a whole lifetime in front of her instead of only a few years, or was it months?

Sometimes Clova would lie awake at night wondering what she could do and where she would go when her mother died.

Then she thought it was selfish to think about herself when her mother was dying, and the only thing that really mattered was that her mother should be happy.

But happiness unfortunately meant spending money, and suddenly Clova found that perhaps through her own stupidity they were down to their last few *francs*.

She was uncomfortably aware that she had refused to face the fact that they were overdrawn at the Bank up to the limit, and there was no chance of their obtaining any more.

She was wondering frantically what she should do, knowing that the rent for the sordid lodgings they were in at the moment was due in a few days time, and there was literally no money to pay for food.

Her mother at the moment appeared to have no admirers willing to provide her with a meal.

"I want a new hat," Lottie said petulantly as Clova helped her to dress.

"That is certainly something we cannot afford, Mama!"

She saw the disappointment in Lottie's still beautiful blue eyes and said:

"I tell you what we will do. The sun is shining and we will walk to the Rue de Rivoli, look at the shops, and pretend we can buy anything we want."

Lottie had laughed spontaneously.

"Yes, that is what we will do," she agreed. "And if I see a kind gentleman friend, I will ask him to give me a new hat. I hate this one!"

"You look very lovely in it, Mama," Clova said.

Because there was that ominous little pink flush in her mother's cheeks, it was the truth.

Last night she had heard her coughing, and she already suspected, although she asked no questions, that Lottie had been coughing blood, but had not said anything to her.

It was a warm Spring day and the chestnut trees were just coming into bloom.

Their lodgings were not in one of the wide, tree-lined roads off the Champs-Élysées, where they had lived in the past, but in a dingy little alleyway, where the houses had deteriorated, and many were condemned as uninhabitable.

It did not take them long, however, to reach the Rue de Rivoli and almost at once Lottie stood entranced in front of a window that was displaying furs.

There was a sable stole with a large number of tails hanging from it, with a muff to match.

"That is what I want!" Lottie cried. "I have wanted one for ages!"

"Then imagine you are wearing it, Mama," Clova said. "Think of it as encircling your shoulders, while your hands are warmed in the muff, then it is yours just as much as if we could afford to pay for it."

Lottie had laughed spontaneously so that several people turned to look at her.

They had moved on, but suddenly Lottie seemed to stagger a little and, afraid she had done too much, Clova put her arm round her.

It took a long time to get home, because Lottie seemed not to have the strength to even put one foot in front of the other.

By the time they reached the dingy house in which

they were living, Clova had practically to carry her up the stairs.

She undressed her mother and put her into bed, then as she fell asleep, Clova went out again.

* * *

The Bank in which Lionel Arkwright had originally opened an account for them was in the Rue Royale.

Clova entered and asked to see the Manager.

Monsieur Beauvais was an elderly man who had been in charge of this branch of the Bank for some years, and Clova knew him.

"I am sorry to bother you, *Monsieur*," she said in her perfect French after he had greeted her, "but my mother is very ill, and although I know we already owe you a small amount of money, I can only beg you to be generous and let us have a further loan."

"I am afraid that is impossible, *Mademoiselle*," he replied. "Much as I would like to accommodate you, it is the policy of Headquarters not to give loans without security, and I must obey their instructions."

"Of course I understand," Clova agreed, "but if you could let us have just a few *louis* for a week or so, I am sure as soon as my mother is better I could pay you back."

"And how would you manage to do that?"

He was thinking as he looked at Clova across his deck how lovely she was.

At the same time, he was well aware that she was far too thin, her chin was sharp against her long neck, and her eyes were too big in her small face for it to be natural.

"I am sure, if nothing else," Clova said slowly, "I

could get a job teaching English to French children, but for the moment I dare not leave my mother."

She had thought out this reply to the question she was sure he would ask, but she was aware as she spoke that it did not sound very convincing.

There was an uncomfortable silence, and she knew the Bank Manager was trying to think how he could put it to her without being too unkind that there was nothing he could do.

Then, as if he played for time, he said:

"All I can promise you, *Mademoiselle*, is that I will write to Headquarters, explain your predicament, and say your mother is a very old customer."

"My mother has banked with you since I was seven," Clova said, remembering that had been her age when she had first come to Paris.

Monsieur Beauvais nodded.

"And now," Clova remarked, "I am nearly nineteen, so we are, as you say, very old customers."

He smiled and stood up.

"I promise I will do my best, *Mademoiselle*, and I will let you know their reply as soon as I can."

There was nothing Clova could do but thank him, and as she walked slowly back she thought despairingly that only a miracle could help her now.

"Please God," she prayed, "send somebody... anybody... anybody... to help Mama. She had not long to... live anyway... and to die of hunger would be too... cruel."

She was still praying when she reached the front door.

The *Concièrge*'s wife, a kindly woman, was just coming out with one of her children in her arms.

"Have you been shopping, *M'mselle*?" she asked.

Clova told her the truth.

"I have no money for shopping, *Madame*. I wish I had. Mama is hungry, and so am I!"

She thought for a moment the woman was going to enquire how in that case she was going to pay the rent, but instead she said:

"There is a little milk and several *croissants* left over from breakfast on the table in my kitchen. If they are of any use, you are welcome to them."

For a moment Clova thought she would kiss the kindly woman, then she said:

"Thank you, *Madame!* Thank you! Thank you! You are very kind, and I know Mama will thank you, too, when I tell her."

She went into the house to find the *croissants* and the milk and hurried up the stairs with them to her mother.

Lottie was still asleep, and Clova thought when she awoke she would break one of the *croissants* into the milk and spoon it to her mother.

She sat in the window, looking out at the sunshine trying to percolate through the gloom of the streets, and wondered what she could do.

"Mama will have to stay in bed tomorrow," she decided, "while I go looking for work."

She saw a flashily dressed woman leave the house opposite and start walking down the street, swinging her hips as she did so, in an unmistakably provocative manner.

It was growing late in the afternoon and Clova knew quite well where she was going.

For a moment it seemed the obvious answer to her own problems, then she shut her eyes in horror at the idea.

Because there was nothing else she could do she started praying again.

* * *

The *croissants* and milk did not seem to interest Lottie much, but what she could not eat kept Clova from lying awake with the pangs of hunger inside her.

She had already looked through their clothes the previous week to see if there was anything more she could sell or pawn, but anything worth even a few *centimes* had already gone.

She walked from her own bedroom across the landing to her mother's, and as she did so she heard the *Concièrge* shouting from down below:

"Is that you, *M'mselle*? There's a letter for you which has just been delivered by hand."

The old man was too fat and lazy to climb the stairs unless he was positively obliged to do so, and Clova knew she would have to fetch the letter herself.

She resisted an impulse to run, knowing that the only person who would have delivered a letter by hand was the Manager of the Bank.

She felt sure it would contain in fulsomely polite tones a refusal to oblige even an old client.

She reached the *Concièrge*'s desk, where he sat in an ancient, dilapidated arm-chair over a small stove, which he kept alight even in the Summer.

"*Voilà, M'mselle,*" he said. "Looks important, doesn't it?"

"Thank you, *Monsieur*, yes, it does!" Clova agreed.

She had no intention of satisfying his curiosity and she walked away without opening the letter until she was half-way up the stairs.

There was a landing, and she went to the window, which badly needed cleaning, and opened the letter which, as she expected, came in an envelope that bore the name of the Bank on the flap.

Slowly she drew out the contents, read the first words, then looked incredulously at the envelope to be quite certain it was her name that was written there.

Mademoiselle Clova McBlane

There was no mistake, and surprisingly "McBlane" was spelled correctly, which was unusual.

She looked at the letter again, then with a cry that seemed to come from the very depths of her heart, she ran up the stairs.

She opened the door to her mother's bedroom and found she was awake, strangely enough looking somehow different from the way she usually did first thing in the morning.

Her hair, despite the touch of grey in it, was golden against the rough cotton pillows, and her eyes seemed to shine as if the sun had caught them.

"Mama! Mama!"

"What . . . is it?" Lottie asked.

With difficulty Clova managed to say:

"Do you remember Jan Maskill?"

There was silence while Lottie thought.

"Should I . . . remember . . . him?

"Yes, Mama. Think! He came from South Africa, a rather good-looking man. He stayed with us for a month here in Paris, and then we went to Monte

Carlo. It must have been five or six years ago."

"Yes—Jan Maskill—of course I...remember him...now," Lottie said. "He loved me...Clova although...he had a...wife and two...tiresome children. He kept...telling me...about them."

Clova looked down at the letter.

"He certainly loved you, Mama! He has died, and left you a fortune!"

Lottie stared at her.

"What do...you mean by...'a fortune'?"

"His Bank has just communicated with ours. The Manager tells me that he had put in your name some shares in his diamond mine."

"Shares?" Lottie said. "I...would rather...have had the...diamonds on my...fingers!"

"You have now inherited the shares on his death," Clova went on, "and they have vastly increased in value. In fact, at the present rate of exchange, they are worth over a million francs."

Clova's voice seemed to break on the last words.

Her mother, however, closed her eyes and there was a happy smile on her lips as she said:

"Now I...can have...those sables—the ones ...I...wanted...yesterday!"

"Yes, of course you can!" Clova agreed.

Her voice broke and the tears were running down her cheeks. But when she could see her mother again, she realised she was dead.

chapter two

LOTTIE was buried with a pomp and style which would have delighted her.

Clova found that the Bank was only too pleased to advance her any amount she required until the money from South Africa arrived and *Monsieur* Beauvais undertook to look after all her affairs.

When the Funeral was over, Clova realised sadly that the only other mourners had been a representative from the Bank and the *Concièrge*'s wife, who had wept copiously through the Service.

It seemed horrifying that Lottie, who had been such a success in Paris when she was with Lionel Arkwright and for many years after he left her, should now have had no one else to mourn her.

As they had gradually become poorer and poorer and moved to shabbier and cheaper accommodations, Lottie had been too proud to contact her old friends.

Moreover, although she would not admit it to herself, she had not felt well enough to make the effort.

But to Clova it seemed bitter that she had not been able to enjoy the money that Jan Maskill had left her.

There had not even been time to buy the sables that had delighted her in the Rue Royale.

Back in the two empty bedrooms after the Funeral was over, Clova looked around her as if she were seeing them for the first time and realised how squalid and uncomfortable they were.

She thought of all the elegant houses and apartments they had lived in before, and knew that those who had disapproved of Lottie would say she had got what she deserved.

Yet it was impossible to forget her laughter, her irresistible enjoyment of life, and the happiness she brought, even if it was a fleeting one, to so many different men.

At least Jan Maskill had appreciated her, and Clova thought that perhaps he and her mother would find happiness together in that other world to which they had travelled within a few weeks of each other.

Now she had to decide what she was going to do, and for the first time she realised how lonely and friendless she was.

She had been so intent on looking after Lottie this last year ever since she had known it was impossible to save her life, that she could hardly remember talking to anyone except shop-assistants and lodging-house keepers.

There was therefore literally no one she could visit in Paris and ask to advise her.

As she thought about it she knew it would be difficult as a young unmarried woman to obtain decent accommodation.

It was unlikely any responsible Hotel would accept her.

She was sure that most Landlords would refuse to let her an apartment when she had no personal credentials and no older woman to chaperon her.

She went to the window to look out over the roofs of Paris and think how frightening it was to be so completely alone and without her mother.

She had loved Lottie with a childlike devotion, and although Lottie had expected her to wait on her hand and foot, she had always felt that by being with her mother she was protected and also had a purpose in life.

Now that was gone and perhaps there would be nothing to replace it.

She put her hands up over her face and instinctively she was praying—fervently—and agonising for help.

Lottie had never felt the need or inclination to attend a Church Service, and living in France, they had not taken the trouble to find a Protestant Church, although it had been a Clergyman from the British Embassy who had taken the Burial Service.

That had been arranged by the Bank Manager, and Clova had only exchanged a few words with the English parson, who was an elderly man with white hair.

Perhaps, Clova thought, she should ask him for assistance; it would certainly be a sensible thing to do.

But it would be embarrassing when he enquired

where she worshipped, and her only answer could be that she and her mother sometimes went into Catholic Churches, lit a candle, and prayed for anything they particularly wanted at that moment.

Clova had the idea that what her mother prayed for was that there would be another man in her life.

She was sure when one did appear that Lottie attributed it to the candle she had lit in the Madeleine, in Notre Dame, or when they were in Monte Carlo, in the Chapel of Ste. Dévote.

"Perhaps I had better wait until tomorrow and ask *Monsieur* Beauvais, who has been so kind and helpful, if he will assist me," Clova decided finally.

Anyway, she had to thank him for everything he had done for her, and it would be easier to call and see him at his office.

She rose from the bed on which she had been sitting and crossed the room to the looking-glass, wiping her eyes as she did so.

One thing she could do would be to buy something decent to wear.

She had bought herself a simple black gown for the Funeral, and now, looking in the mirror, she thought her mother had been right when she said that because of their fair hair and blue eyes and translucent white skin, black made both of them look theatrical.

Not that that had worried Lottie. Indeed, she often added a black gown to the expensive garments she purchased when some man was paying for them

But black, sparkling with *diamanté*, ornamented with flowers and feathers was very different from the severe black of mourning.

As Clova looked at her reflection she had the uncomfortable feeling that if she tried to find a position as a teacher in a School or as a Governess in a Parisian household, her employer would think she looked too sensational, or perhaps "flamboyant" was the right word.

"I will not wear black," she decided, knowing that if Lottie knew why she did not appear in mourning, she would think it sensible, and not in the least insulting to herself.

"One must always make the best of one's-self," her mother had said not once but a hundred times as they moved about Paris or journeyed to Monte Carlo.

"No one could suggest that you do anything else, Mama," Clova had answered.

"But you have not combed your hair properly this morning, and your shoes are dusty," Lottie had replied. "Appearances are always important, and I would not want any of my friends to think I neglected my little daughter."

It was only as the years passed and Clova grew older and more mature that Lottie would make excuses to keep her in the background.

"I am lunching with a delightful gentleman who asked me to bring you with me," she would say, "but I know, darling, you would find it boring, listening to us talking about ourselves, or rather, he talking about me. So I am sure you would rather have luncheon in our Sitting-Room."

"Yes, of course, Mama," Clova would agree.

She was no longer the little girl with golden curls who was an asset to Lottie's beauty and to Lottie's sparkling gaiety.

She had become a woman, and Lottie had no wish, although Clova liked to think she had not ex-

25

pressed it even to herself, to find a rival in her own daughter.

But it had not been necessary for the last six months to keep out of sight of Lottie's admirers, for there had not been any and she had none of her own.

"I have to do something," she told herself desperately, and knew it was the Bank Manager to whom she must turn for help.

She looked at the hard, uncomfortable iron bedstead in which she had been sleeping, at the wallpaper which was peeling from the walls, and the curtains that would not pull completely across the window, and decided that, when there was no necessity for it, she could not bear to stay here any longer.

She was also vividly conscious of the empty room across the passage, where her mother had died.

She knew crying would not bring her back. She had to start a new life on her own, and the sooner she got down to business the better.

She thought *Monsieur* Beauvais would be back in his office at about three o'clock, having, like most Frenchman, doubtless enjoyed a long luncheon with perhaps a number of other business associates or with a pretty woman.

"I will go to the Bank now," Clova decided.

She put on the plain black hat she had worn for the Funeral and started to walk down the uncarpeted stairs.

As she reached the bottom she saw a man standing at the desk speaking to the *Concièrge*.

"I am calling on Miss Clova McBlane," he said in English.

He had a strange accent and the *Concièrge*, heaving himself out of his arm-chair with some difficulty, replied:

"*Pardon, Monsieur, qu'est-ce qu'il vous faut?*"

"Miss McBlane!" the man replied in a slightly louder tone.

Clova walked towards him.

"I am Clova McBlane," she said in English.

The man turned from the desk.

He was elderly, with hair and side-whiskers that were turning white, and dressed, she thought, in a severe fashion which made her think he was perhaps a Minister of some sort.

"You are Clova McBlane?" he asked as if he must make sure of her identity.

Clova nodded and smiled.

"I was told I would find you here," he said, "but I thought I must be mistaken."

Clova knew without his saying so that he was appalled by the sordidness of the entrance, the worn and none-too-clean linoleum on the stairs, and walls that had not been painted for at least a dozen years.

For a moment she felt she must apologise for being found in such unpleasant surroundings.

Then pride made her lift her chin a little before she asked:

"May I enquire why you are here?"

"Yes, of course," her visitor answered. "Is there somewhere where we can talk?"

Clova knew she could not ask him upstairs either to her mother's empty bedroom or her own.

She looked through the open door at the sunshine outside.

"I was just going for a walk," she said. "It is not

far to the Champs-Élysées, where we can find a seat under the trees."

She thought the strange man was about to argue with her, then asked quickly, feeling she should have done so before:

"Perhaps you should tell me your name?"

"It is the same as yours. I am Torbot McBlane."

Clova stared at him in astonishment.

It flashed through her mind that he must be a relation, and almost as if he could read her thoughts, he said quickly:

"I am, My Lady, one of the Elders of your Clan!"

Clova was bewildered. She had hardly thought of her father or of the Clan since she and her mother had left Scotland.

There had been so much that was new to fascinate her when she had first come to Paris that she had hardly spared a thought for her grandfather's Castle looming over the Strath: the moors stretching out behind it, or of their own small rather ugly house, the gloom of which had only seemed enlivened by her mother.

Now she wondered why Torbot McBlane was here, then knew the answer without his telling her.

"I think," she said slowly, "that you have come to tell me that my father is dead."

"Yes, that is the truth. The Marquess died over a month ago."

"The Marquess?" Clova exclaimed. "Do you mean my grandfather?"

Torbot McBlane shook his head.

"No, the old Marquess died six years ago. You did not hear of it?"

"I am afraid not."

"It was your father who succeeded him."

"And Uncle Rory?"

"He was drowned at sea soon after you and your mother left."

Clova knew now why Torbot McBlane had addressed her as "My Lady."

If on her grandfather's death her father had succeeded to the Marquessate, she would have become Lady Clova McBlane, while her mother, because she and her father had never been divorced, would have been the Marchioness of Strathblane.

She wondered if it would have made any difference to Lottie's last years, when they had had so little money and their friends had gradually deserted them.

But it was too late to worry about that now.

She realised that the *Concièrge*, although unable to understand what they were saying, was staring at them with curiosity, and she said firmly to Torbot McBlane:

"Let us find somewhere where we can sit down."

He obviously thought it strange, but there was nothing he could do but agree.

They walked quickly and in silence down the narrow street, and crossing the Boulevard at the end of it, came in a short time to the chestnut trees which bordered the Champs-Élysées.

As Clova expected, there were children bowling their hoops and running over the grass, nurses gossiping together while their charges slept in their expensive prams.

There was also an old man selling red-and-white balloons, which furnished a brilliant patch of colour against the greenery and the silver fountains playing in the Place de la Concorde.

Clova saw a seat that was unoccupied and sitting down on it looked up at Torbot McBlane, who, lifting his coat-tails, sat beside her.

"Now, Mr. McBlane," she said. "Tell me why you are here."

"I thought you would have known before now, My Lady, of your grandfather's death."

"I am afraid there is little written about Scotland in the French newspapers," Clova replied.

"You have lived in France ever since you left us?" Torbot McBlane enquired.

"Yes, either in Paris or in other parts of France."

She did not mention Monte Carlo, knowing that to the Scots it would seem a den of iniquity.

She was well aware that some French newspapers, like the English ones, denounced the Casino as a "hell on earth."

She and her mother had often laughed at the letters that had been written against the evils of gambling and the suicides that resulted from it.

"It may be a stupid way of dying," Lottie had said once, "but at least the poor devils have some fun for their money, which is more than one can say of those who never swerve from the path of righteousness!"

It was the sort of remark that made the men who escorted Lottie roar with laughter and compliment her on her wit.

But Clova had thought, when Lottie sold or pawned her jewels because she insisted on going gambling without a man to pay for her losses, that it was a fool's way of spending money.

Torbot McBlane was talking slowly and ponderously

"When your grandfather died your father became the Chieftain of the Clan. A fine man he was, a born leader, and we miss him sorely."

There was just a touch of emotion in his voice, which made Clova say softly:

"I am sorry that I did not know him... better."

There was a silence, then she asked:

"Did he ever... speak of me?"

"He was not a man to express his feelings aloud," Torbot McBlane replied, "but we knew he was thinking of you when he sat alone in the Castle, and there was no family to cheer him, or to talk to him when his day's work was done."

There was a pause as he finished speaking, and Clova could only say again:

"I... I am sorry."

"All the Clan will miss him," Torbot McBlane went on, "and without his guidance we will be like sheep without a shepherd, until the new Chieftain takes his place."

"I can understand that," Clova said, "and who is your new Chieftain?"

Torbot McBlane turned to look at her and there was something very solemn in his expression, and his voice was like the voice of doom as he said:

"It is you, My Lady!"

Clova stared at him wide-eyed.

"Me? What do you mean?"

"Your father had no son, and in Scotland a female can inherit. You are therefore now the Marchioness of Strathblane and Chieftain of our Clan!"

For a moment Clova could not breathe, then she said:

"I... I do not... believe it!"

"It is true, and that is why I have come to Paris, to beg you to come back because our people need you."

Clova could only stare at him speechless.

Then she turned away to look at the children playing under the trees, the sunshine percolating through the branches and leaves to cast a yellow pattern on the grass.

She felt that what she was seeing was burnt in her mind, and she would always remember it.

In a voice that did not seem like her own she asked:

"Is . . . is it possible for me to . . . go back after . . . I have been . . . with my . . . away for so long?"

Torbot McBlane was obviously aware of what she had been about to say and he replied:

"The past is past, My Lady. It is the future that matters, and the future of the Clan is in your keeping."

"What can I do?"

"You can come back to your home where you belong and to the people who are waiting for you."

His answer seemed to decide everything, and Clova knew there would be no argument about it.

* * *

Looking out of the window of the train that was carrying her to Glasgow, Clova was aware that Torbot McBlane had taken charge of her as if it were he who was the Chieftain rather than herself.

He had found first a quiet, respectable Hotel in Paris where they could stay.

After Clova had collected the few things that had belonged to her mother and herself which she wished to keep, she had told him that she could not leave for Scotland until she had some decent clothes to wear.

There was no need to explain that she had been desperately poor until a few days ago when she had learned of her mother's windfall from South Africa.

Torbot McBlane had learnt exactly what had happened from the Bank Manager.

It was the Chief of Police whom he had contacted in the first place who had informed him that Lottie was dead and everything appertaining to her Funeral had been arranged by *Monsieur* Beauvais.

Clova could understand that the Funeral had attracted attention.

She was to find the following morning there was a description of it in the French newspapers, which included the information that although Lottie had been known as *"Mme. McBlane,"* she was in actual fact the Marchioness of Strathblane.

The Press had found out who she was, while neither she nor her mother had the slightest idea that her father had inherited the title some years earlier.

"I had expected it would take a long time to find you, My Lady," Torbot McBlane explained, "and it was the hand of Providence that I was able to do so so quickly."

Although he had never been abroad before, he had travelled widely in Scotland and was, Clova found, extremely well-read.

He was a farmer in quite a large way on her father's estate and a respected Elder of the Clan, and had been deputed by the others to undertake the somewhat formidable task of finding Clova after her father's death.

She had the feeling, although Torbot McBlane never said so, that it was a merciful relief to him to learn that her mother was dead.

Although they never spoke of it, Clova felt sure the Clan would never forgive Lottie for running away and for taking her child with her.

She thought now that it must have been hard on her father, dour and dull though he might have been, to be left alone.

He could never marry again without obtaining a divorce, which was a difficult procedure, and in his position unthinkable. He therefore had no hope of having the male heir he must have longed for.

"I suppose it was wrong of Mama to leave him," Clova told herself.

But she knew, thinking back, which was difficult to do, that Lottie was like a butterfly in a cage and it had been impossible to stop her from spreading her wings and escaping.

After Clova had bought the clothes which she hoped would be suitable for Scotland, she told Torbot McBlane she was ready for the journey ahead of them.

She had hurried as quickly as she could to buy herself what was a complete wardrobe, knowing that nothing she had before was worth keeping, for otherwise she would have undoubtedly sold or pawned it.

Anyway, what was suitable for Paris would certainly look outrageous on a Scottish moor.

She was not quite certain what in fact would be suitable, but she had taken the advice of the best shops in Paris.

Although of course even their plainest gowns had a *chic* and an elegance about them that was different from anything she was likely to find in Scotland, Clova knew with satisfaction that they made her look not only beautiful, but without question a Lady.

She had the feeling, as she spent the money that the Bank Manager was only too willing to lend her, that she was perhaps indulging herself for the last time.

Torbot McBlane was already telling her of the difficulties she would find in Scotland, the unemployment amongst many of the Clan, and the complexities of successfully breeding sheep who had little to feed on.

Then there were the Highland cattle that never appeared to grow fat.

Clova listened carefully to everything he had to say.

She felt woefully ignorant and more and more afraid of failing those who she understood expected so much from her.

"Surely," she said as they journeyed North, "there must be somebody else, a man, a near relative, who would be more suitable as your Chieftain than a woman?"

"To us you are rightful heir for the position," Torbot McBlane said firmly, "even though there are some who would push themselves forward."

This is what Clova expected to hear, and she asked:

"So there are other aspirants for the Chieftainship! Who are they?"

She thought for a moment that Torbot McBlane was not going to reply. Then he said:

"There is one in particular and we do not want him."

"By 'we' do you mean the Elders, or the Clan?"

"Both!"

"Then who is he?"

35

Torbot McBlane's lips tightened for a moment and there was an expression in his eyes which Clova thought was quite intimidating.

"He is a distant Cousin of yours."

"And what is the name of this distant Cousin?"

"He is called Euan McBlane."

"And you say that he wishes to be Chieftain?"

"It is what he wishes, but when he offered himself, the Elders told him firmly that he was not eligible while your father had a daughter alive."

Clova was silent.

The tone of Torbot McBlane's voice told her there was something more behind all this, and after a moment she asked:

"Why do you so much dislike my Cousin?"

There was a long silence, and she thought she would not receive a reply, until finally Torbot McBlane said:

"He was educated in the South and came back to Scotland despising the land of his birth and praising our enemies, the English, who have done nothing for us, and whose cruelties, when we fought against them, will never be forgotten!"

The way Torbot McBlane spoke was like a call to arms, and Clova could only ask a little nervously:

"Are the old feelings and feuds still as prevalent as they were in the past?"

"The Scots never forget or forgive," Torbot McBlane answered.

"Surely you realise that I am half-English?" Clova said. "My mother, as you know, came from Yorkshire."

"It is your father that counts. He was a McBlane, he lived and he died as one. That is what we remember, and it is his blood which will guide you and show you the way."

He might have been the Prophet Isaiah speaking to his people, Clova thought.

Because she was curious she said:

"Tell me more about my Cousin Euan. Surely you cannot condemn him completely because he was educated in England?"

"He would rather live there, which he cannot afford to do, than with us."

The explanation was sharp, almost curt, and Clova had the feeling that it hurt Torbot McBlane even to speak of her Cousin.

After a moment she said:

"I hope I will not start off a war against anyone, least of all against those who are relatives."

She thought as she spoke that it would be pleasant to have relatives so she could belong somewhere.

Perhaps as time went by they would learn to love her, and she would not feel so alone and helpless as she did at the moment.

As if Torbot McBlane could again sense what she was feeling, he began to talk to her of the history of the McBlanes: of the battles they had fought in the past, the miseries they had suffered during the Clearances, when they had been turned out of their homes and from the land on which they had been born.

Many of them had been sent cruelly across the seas to Canada, where a great number had died at the hands of the Indians, or from starvation because they could not find work.

As he spoke, it all seemed to come back to Clova as if she had heard it before, or else it had been dormant in her mind.

Now she could remember many things she had forgotten, and which she had never thought about once they had receded into the mists of the past.

Most of all, she could recall the huge Castle with its large rooms, and her grandfather, magnificent and awe-inspiring in his kilt, his tasselled sporran, and plaid caught on the shoulder.

Could she really take his place?

It seemed impossible, and she wanted to jump out of the train, leave Torbot McBlane, and go back to Paris or anywhere in France, which was far more home to her than the bleakness of what lay ahead in Scotland.

"I cannot do it!" she told herself. "I cannot face the people with whom I have nothing in common, except that I was born amongst them."

Why could they not accept her Cousin Euan McBlane as their Chieftain?

What was wrong with them that there should have been such a sharp note in Torbot's voice when he spoke of him?

"The whole thing is ridiculous!" she told herself.

Yet as Torbot went on talking, she could not help feeling proud that the McBlanes had fought so valiantly against the English, and that the Castle had stood for five centuries.

The Marchioness of Strathblane!

Was it possible that that was who she was now?

It seemed so incredible, she wanted to laugh at the mere idea of it.

Yet she knew it was true when they had reached Edinburgh and boarded the ship which was to carry them to Inverness.

She knew from the way she was greeted by the

attendants that the best accommodation was accorded her by right.

For the first time in her life she had become a person of importance; a person other people respected.

Only when she was alone in her cabin and Torbot McBlane was marching round the deck for exercise did she laugh to herself because it all seemed so absurd.

'If only Mama were here,' she thought, 'what fun we should have!'

Then she knew that if she was truthful, Lottie would scandalise someone like Torbot McBlane because she would treat everything so lightly.

She would doubtless poke fun at the solemnity with which he spoke of the McBlanes, their history, and the traditions which surrounded the Chieftain.

"It was all so boring, darling," she had said often enough to Clova when they spoke of Scotland. "They all take themselves so seriously. No one laughs."

She laughed herself before she went on.

"I fell in love with Lionel because his eyes twinkled, and when your father was droning on about some misfortune that had happened to one of the Clan, I knew Lionel was thinking, as I was, that there was nothing more deadly than other people's troubles."

'No, even if she was the Marchioness, Mama would not have wanted to go back,' Clova thought now.

At the same time, she would have been in a very different position with money to spend, money which came from the Diamond Mines of South Africa. Money that was hers!

Clova had not missed the respect with which Torbot McBlane had spoken of her new-found wealth.

"It is fine that you have money of your own, My Lady," he said. "Your father found it hard to refuse the many requests for help which came to him, but he was a just man, and he did what he could for those who deserved help."

Clova could almost see her father and the Elders investigating each case and deciding whether it was a worthy one, or whether the applicant should be sent away penniless.

She had the feeling that if it was left to her in the future, she would need every penny of the money Jan Maskill had left her mother, and a great deal more besides.

Almost insidiously the idea came to her that it would be far simpler and far more enjoyable for her to go back to Paris.

She could lead a life of her own amongst the French, as her mother had done, even though socially she had been under a cloud for having left her husband.

'I could start without any impediment,' Clova thought. 'I could find somebody to chaperon me who was respectable, perhaps an aristocrat who had fallen on hard times, and I would soon be invited to parties, Balls, and Receptions and make new friends, and eventually... who knows? I might marry a Frenchman!'

It was the call of the life she had known. The life that had moments of glamour, or had seemed so when she was a child, looking at it now from outside and yet, because she was Lottie's daughter, as a part of it.

Then almost as if Torbot McBlane were speaking to her, she knew that her duty was to do what her father's Clan asked of her, which was to take his place.

She would find people to instruct her, people to tell her what was expected.

Yet as she journeyed from France to Scotland, it had seemed, as she looked back, that Paris was brilliant with light and laughter, while Scotland was dark, grey, dour, and gloomy.

She drew in her breath.

Then as she felt propellors of the Steamship revolving in the grey waters, she told herself that if the worse came to the worst she would run away.

At least, unlike Lottie, she did not need anyone to pay for her—she could pay for herself.

chapter three

It took a long time to reach Inverness, where they stayed the night before starting out early in the morning by carriage, which was to carry them to the Castle.

It was a well-sprung travelling-carriage, drawn by four stalwart horses, which Clova learnt had been sent to Inverness to await their arrival.

To her surprise Torbot McBlane did not step inside with her, but sat on the box with the coachman because, as he told her, he wanted fresh air.

She had the feeling he was also rather bored at having to make conversation and was by nature a quiet man who seldom expressed his feelings.

She was sure that was true of all Scots.

It had been the trouble with her father, who doubtless never paid her mother the fulsome compliments which she had so much enjoyed receiving from the French.

As soon as they were out of the town, Clova began to have her first glimpse of the Scottish countryside.

Now there were hills in the distance, and as they drove alongside a large expanse of water, she was not certain whether it was a loch or an inlet of the sea.

It was all very lovely, with the trees green against barren rocks, and the sunshine touching everything with gold.

She had the feeling that the sky seemed larger than it had when she was in France, and in fact everything had a freshness and an untouched natural beauty which kept her bending towards the open window in case she should miss anything.

They drove for nearly two hours before they changed horses, which also Clova learnt had come from the Castle.

Then after a short time they set off again.

Now the road became narrower and at times very steep, until when Clova was beginning to feel hungry they came to a stop after a climb which had made the horses sweat.

Torbot McBlane got down from the box and came to the carriage-door and opened it.

"I thought, My Lady," he said, "you would like to have luncheon here and rest the horses before we start down the hill which will eventually lead us to the Castle."

"How far away is it?" Clova asked.

"About an hour's drive," he replied, "but they will

not be expecting you until the middle of the afternoon."

He seemed to have it all planned, so Clova was glad to get out of the carriage and stretch her legs.

It was then she realised how magnificent the view was which lay beneath her.

They were high up on a moor, and below she could see the coast of Scotland, rugged with its inlets, melting away into the misty horizon.

The sea was vividly blue in the sunshine, even bluer, she thought, than the Mediterranean, and just below, winding through heather-covered banks, was a small river flowing down to the sea.

It was so beautiful that Clova caught her breath, and once again was conscious of that sensation of ecstasy, almost painful in its intensity, which beauty always gave her.

As she stood, half-afraid it might vanish in front of her eyes, Torbot McBlane and the two coachmen unpacked a hamper which had been attached on top of her luggage at the back of the carriage.

They spread a rug against a rough cairn on which they could lean, and arranged in front of it dishes of cold meats, eggs cooked inside baked potatoes, and a salad of lettuce, carrots, and young beetroots.

There were scones and a large pat of golden butter besides a piece of cheese that to Clova's eyes was curiously pink.

"I thought, My Lady, you would not need much," Torbot McBlane said apologetically, "as you will be having a large dinner tonight."

"A large dinner?" she questioned.

"Yes," he answered, "your relatives will be gathering at the Castle to greet you, and tomorrow the Clansmen will come from all parts to pay homage to our new Chieftain."

"You did not tell me this before," Clova said.

He gave her an apologetic smile, but there was an undoubted twinkle in his eye as he explained:

"I did not want to frighten you!"

"But I am frightened," Clova replied, "in case I should do something wrong."

"There will be plenty of people to prevent you from doing that," he said dryly, and waited for her to sit down.

The coachman tactfully drew away, and Clova felt she was isolated in this strange land, which she had to admit was very much more beautiful than she had anticipated.

In fact she could not help feeling there was something familiar about it; something which made her feel she had come home to where she belonged, although such a thought seemed disloyal to her mother.

Then she told herself that if she intended to stay, then the sooner she remembered the importance of her Scottish blood and forgot she was half-English, the better.

Because she was hungry and had been too tired last night after the long voyage to eat much, she enjoyed every mouthful of the picnic which Torbot McBlane had provided for her.

He had included for her fresh lemonade while he himself drank a bottle of beer.

When they had finished he said:

"There is no hurry. We got here quicker than I expected, and I do not want you to arrive at the Castle until they are ready to receive you."

Clova smiled.

"In that case, I am going to walk a little way over the heather."

She knew from the way he settled himself firmly against the stone cairn that he had no wish to accompany her, and she walked away finding sheep-tracks through the heather which carried her down hill.

She was still quite a long way from the river when she saw in the distance a man in a kilt running along the bank, and for a few seconds she could not understand the reason for his haste.

Then she saw that he was carrying a fishing-rod which was bent and knew he was following a salmon.

It was over eleven years since she had last seen a man fishing for salmon, yet now it came back to her and instinctively she hurried as quickly as she could down towards the river.

By the time she reached it, the fisherman was no longer running, but standing ready to reel in a large salmon that was fighting frantically to escape.

There was the noise of the reel as his captor drew him steadily in, and then as the fish leapt in the air, Clova saw it was fresh in from the sea, and in her eyes very large.

She reached the fisherman and stood behind him watching how expertly he handled the fish.

As it jumped again in a desperate attempt to break loose, he dipped the point of the rod and let the line run out.

Clova did not speak, but he must have been aware that she was there because as he started again to draw the salmon towards the bank he said sharply: "Can you gaff him for me?"

As he spoke Clova saw that a gaff was attached to his belt which encircled his waist above his kilt.

She moved nearer, then realising that if she had to gaff the fish, she would have to scramble quite a distance down the bank and perhaps even stand in the shallow water beneath it.

"I am afraid I cannot do what you ask," she said tentatively. "I might lose your fish."

"Very well," he said impatiently, as if he thought she was extremely stupid. "Hold the rod for me, and if he jumps again, do not forget to lower the point."

He passed the rod into her hands without looking at her, and taking the gaff from his belt, climbed down the side of the bank.

"Reel him in gently," he ordered. "Gently! Keep his head up and step back—go on—step back!"

His voice sharpened as she took a second to follow his instructions.

Then leaning out he thrust the shining silver point of the gaff into the side of the salmon and lifted him out of the water.

He landed the fish on the bank, then climbed up to hold it down where it lay thrashing its tail on the rough grass, and hit it sharply on the head with the handle of the gaff.

The salmon was dead, and now Clova could see the fisherman was an exceedingly handsome young man with clear-cut features, dark brown hair, and a sunburnt skin that appeared to have almost a golden glow about it.

He removed the hook from the fish's mouth, and for the first time looked up at Clova, who was standing holding the rod in her hand.

She had taken off her bonnet while eating luncheon, and her hair was in the sunshine, a halo of gold, and her blue eyes were very large in her pointed face, but shining with excitement at what she had just seen.

The fisherman stared at her in astonishment for some seconds before he said:

"Are you real? I thought you were one of the shepherds who had come down to help me."

"I am glad I was able to do so."

"I am very grateful, and as you see, we have landed a very fine catch!"

"What do you think he weighs?" Clova asked.

"Between twelve and fourteen pounds!"

Clova gave a little exclamation and he added:

"At least it will 'keep the wolf from the door' for a few days!"

Clova smiled.

"I cannot believe there are many wolves in such a beautiful place!"

"Not animals," the fisherman corrected her, "but human beings who behave like wolves, jackals, and poisonous snakes!"

He spoke with such bitterness in his voice that Clova asked curiously:

"What do you mean? How can there be people like that when everything around them is so lovely?"

"That is what I asked myself when I came back," the fisherman replied.

Again there was a note in his voice which made Clova ask:

"What has upset you?"

She spoke impulsively, without thinking that perhaps she was intruding on something private and it might seem impertinent from a stranger.

"If you want the truth," the fisherman said as he rose to his feet, "this morning I found two of my best ewes, for which I paid more than I could really afford, lying dead on the moor with their throats cut!"

Clova gave a cry of horror.

"Who could have done such a thing? Who could have been so cruel?"

"It is easy to answer that!" the fisherman replied. "An enemy who strikes at night when he cannot be seen, leaving no trace of his identity, although it is not hard to know who he is."

"I do not understand," Clova said. "Why should you have an enemy like that here? What have you done to provoke him?"

"What have I done?" the fisherman enquired. "Nothing except belong to a Clan which is forced, if they are to survive, to fight a ridiculous war against those who are waging an age-old feud against their fellow-Scots instead of uniting and trying to bring Scotland into a new age."

There was silence for a moment until Clova said:

"Are you saying that your sheep have been slaughtered by members of another Clan?"

"Of course that is what I am saying," the fisherman replied impatiently, "and the idiots do not understand that they are not only injuring me and my people, but themselves! Who would invest money in new industries in a country that is steeped in the feuds and prejudices of the Middle Ages?"

He spoke so violently that Clova drew in her breath. Then he said quickly:

"Forgive me, I should not be talking to you like this. I can see you are a tourist coming farther North than most of them do to laugh at the quaint customs of backward people!"

Now he was speaking mockingly, and Clova replied quietly:

"That is not true."

The fisherman smiled, and it seemed to transform his face.

"I can think of no other explanation," he said, "why anybody so beautiful and so exquisitely dressed should appear suddenly to help me when I most wanted help, unless of course you have dropped down from the sky."

"I certainly came a long way down the moor to assist you." Clova smiled.

She glanced back to where she had come from, and as the fisherman's eyes followed hers he could see the carriage and horses waiting at the top of the hill.

"I see now that I have interrupted your journey," he said. "I suppose, if I behaved correctly, I should offer you this salmon as a reward for your labours."

"No, no, of course not," Clova said quickly. "You said that you needed it yourself, and it would keep you from being hungry."

She thought as she spoke of how often she had been hungry before her mother had died, and how much she had disliked scanty and poor-quality food, which was all they could afford.

"Perhaps you have a family waiting for you."

The fisherman smiled again.

"If you are asking if I am married, the answer is 'no,' I cannot afford to be. But you have not yet told me about yourself. What is your name?"

"Clova."

"A Scottish name? But you do not look like a Scot, and most of the women around here are dark-haired like their Pictish ancestors, or red-headed."

"My Godmother came from the Grampian Mountains."

"Is that where you have come from?"

She was just about to tell him the truth, that she had come from France, but instead she said:

"You have not told me your name."

"I apologise. I should have introduced myself. I am Tarquil, the Laird of Cowan, for what it is worth, ruling over a Castle that is falling more and more into disrepair with every wind that blows, and a Clan that has lost heart through privation and the injuries perpetrated on it by our neighbours."

"The Kilcowans!" Clova murmured to herself.

Somehow she could hear the name being spoken of when she was small.

"Yes, the Kilcowans," the Laird said aggressively. "A proud Clan, although we are of no importance to anyone except ourselves."

"And who are your enemies," Clova asked, "those who killed your ewes?"

She knew the answer before he spoke.

"Who but the McBlanes?" he answered. "They have been determined for the last three hundred years to exterminate us, and now are within reach of achieving their objective."

Although there was a bitterness in his voice, when he finished speaking he smiled again and said:

"I am boring you with my troubles, and I can only excuse myself by saying you are the first person I have spoken to since I found my ewes dead, and realised that once again I had thrown away what little money I had on trying to make a living for my people by improving the breed of our own sheep."

As Clova would have answered him there was a shout from the road high up above them, and she looked up to see Torbot McBlane waving to her.

"I have to go," she said, "but I would like to see you again, if it is possible, and I promise I will try to help you to put an end to these ridiculous feuds that should have died out long ago in a civilised country."

"*You* will help me?" he asked.

Then as she looked up into the dark eyes that seemed to her to penetrate below the surface as if he were looking for something very special, he said quietly:

"Because I cannot believe you are real, because you appeared to help me when I am quite certain I could not have managed that salmon without you, I am prepared to believe, although it seems incredible, what you have said."

"I said I would try," Clova answered in a very low voice.

She did not know why, but though he had not moved, she had the feeling that they were touching each other, and she felt as if her whole body vibrated to him.

It was a strange, unaccountable feeling that she had never had before. But it was very real and she was vividly conscious of him.

She was aware of his broad shoulders, the open-necked shirt he wore without a coat, his kilt that was faded, yet became him in a manner which she was certain no other garment could do, and his eyes dark in his sun-burnt face.

"You are very lovely," he said, looking down at her, "and I am afraid, if I let you go, I shall never see you again! However, when I asked you if you were real, you said you were. So how can I find you?"

Clova drew in her breath.

"I am on my way to the Castle of Strathblane!"

She saw the expression on the Laird's face change.

"I do not believe it! Clova! But of course, you are the Marchioness's daughter, and you have been brought back from France."

"You have heard of me?"

"The whole countryside is talking about you, and saying you will be the new Chieftain."

There was a twist to his lips as he said:

"May I be the first to welcome you in your new position, to the territory over which you will rule, and the people who will obey you."

He paused before he went on:

"You said you hoped to see me again, but I think that is unlikely. They will not allow you to fraternise with the enemy, for make no mistake, My Lady, the McBlanes hate and loathe the Kilcowans, and would exterminate them all if they could."

Somehow Clova felt hypnotised by what he was saying, then throwing out her hands as if she were protecting herself physically, she cried:

"No! No! You are wrong to think like that! It is wicked and something I shall not allow. If my people are menacing yours, I will prevent them from doing so. As you say, we are living in a new era. We must become civilised; we must advance as other countries all over Europe are advancing."

The Laird stared at her.

"Are you really saying this to me?" he asked. "How can you think as you do?"

"It is how any sensible person would think."

"I agree with you, but you will find it hard to make anybody around you understand it. They will believe you are speaking in a foreign language!"

"Then we must make them understand!" Clova said firmly.

"'We'?"

He raised his eyebrows.

"Are you suggesting that you and I will fight this formidable campaign together?"

"Why not? If we have any authority, then our Clans should listen to us," Clova said, "and we have to tell them what is wrong and what is right."

The Laird drew in his breath.

"That is the way the Scots should be thinking and talking," he said quickly. "Oh, my dear, I only pray that you will not become disillusioned, as I have been."

"Are you really prepared to give up so easily?" Clova asked. "We have to convince our people, if no one else, that feuds and warring among the Clans is dangerously out of date. You may laugh at me, but I cannot help thinking that the real enemy of Scotland is a hard fact of economics. The country lacks money."

The Laird stared at her. Then he said:

"You are not real! No woman as young as you could think like that, but because I am prepared to follow you to Heaven or Hell, I pledge my allegiance."

He looked at her for a long moment, then he went down on one knee, and taking her hand kissed it.

55

Clova knew it was the age-old obeisance given by tribesmen to the Chieftain of their Clan, but as he took her hand she could not help her fingers tightening on his.

He rose to his feet, and now he seemed to tower above her.

"If you need me," he said, "send for me, and I will come to you. But because I value my life, I prefer that it should be in the daytime rather than at night."

"Are you really... suggesting that my people might... kill you?"

"There is certainly one amongst them who would not hesitate to do so."

Clova was still. Then, although she knew the answer, she had to ask the question.

"Are you... speaking of my... Cousin Euan McBlane?"

"So you have been told about him!"

"Yes, and I intend to judge him for myself."

"I hope you will do that, but remember he is a dangerous man, and he wants above all things to be the Chieftain of the McBlanes."

"Are you... suggesting that he might try to... kill me?"

There was a twist to the Laird's lips before he replied:

"He has a better idea than that and has already been talking about it quite freely."

"And what is that?"

"He intends to marry you!"

Clova stared at him in sheer astonishment.

"To... marry me?"

"Why not? He will then be almost in the position

he desires, and if you should die accidentally, which of course would be very regrettable, he would be too firmly ensconced for anybody to be able to oust him from the throne."

Clova did not speak, and after a moment the Laird said in a different tone:

"I should not be frightening you, but I want you to promise me one thing."

"What is . . . that?"

Clova's voice was hardly above a whisper.

"If you really are frightened by anything that occurs to make you think that you are in danger, you will let me know."

Clova nodded.

"I will do that."

There was another shout from the ridge above her, and she said:

"I have to go now."

"Of course, and I will return to my own land and think about you."

He smiled as he added:

"Incidentally, at the moment I am poaching on McBlane territory! Our boundary is a good quarter-of-a-mile farther up the river."

"So we really are neighbours?"

"Neighbours with a sword, or rather a dirk, keeping us apart."

"That is something I shall not allow to happen," Clova said firmly. "You are my first friend in Scotland, and I do not intend to lose you!"

"If that is the truth, it makes me feel very proud."

"It is true, and I am also rather frightened. I know very little about the land I left when I was only seven years old."

The Laird smiled.

"You will find those first seven years were very important, and now that you are home again you will remember what you thought you had forgotten. Scotland and the call of the Highlands will ring in your ears, beat in your heart, throb through your blood, and you cannot escape from it!"

"Is that what you have found?"

"Exactly! And that is why you will find there is no escape, and even if there were, you would not take it."

Again what he was saying seemed hypnotic.

Then as Torbot McBlane shouted for the third time, Clova forced herself to walk away.

"Au revoir!"

The French farewell, which was so much more explicit than "good-bye," came instinctively to her lips.

As if he understood, the Laird said in reply:

"Au revoir, beautiful Chieftain of the McBlanes. I swear, however difficult it may seem, that I shall see you soon."

Clova smiled at him, then she was running up the tiny, twisting sheep-tracks to where Torbot McBlane was waiting for her impatiently.

They arrived at the Castle as the sun was sinking a little and the shadows were growing longer.

It was then, as she saw the Castle, large, imposing, magnificent, rising above the Strath, silhouetted against a protective circle of green fir-trees, above which rose the barren tops of the moors, that she realized how impressive it was.

There was a river running down the middle of the Strath, the hills on each side seeming designed as a background for the authority of the Castle.

The horses turned in through some large iron gates, and then as they went a little farther up the drive, Clova could hear the sound of the pipes.

It was the tune the McBlane pipers played when going to war which greeted her as she drew nearer and nearer and saw four Pipers standing outside the great oak door.

There was also a group of Clansmen who, she thought before Torbot McBlane confirmed that she was right, were the servants who worked in the gardens, the foresters and game-keepers from the forests, the gillies from the river and the stalkers, who had come down from the hills.

Torbot McBlane had driven in the carriage with her for the last few miles of her journey in order to explain who would be the guests waiting to greet her when she arrived.

They would all be close relatives who had come from various outlying parts of the estate, where they had houses or Castles of their own, but were extremely proud of being an intimate part of the Chieftain's family.

He did not at first mention Euan McBlane, and when he had completed long descriptions of the other relatives, Clova enquired:

"And will my Cousin Euan McBlane be there?"

She thought that Torbot McBlane's face darkened before he replied:

"He will be there! You may be certain of that, My Lady."

"I would like you to speak frankly about him," Clova said. "Why do you dislike him and why are the Elders so determined that he should not be their Chieftain?"

"As I have already told you, he has no real fondness for Scotland."

"I think there is more to it than that," Clova protested.

Torbot McBlane did not speak, and after a moment she said:

"Is he intent on furthering the feuds between us and the Clans who live on the borders of our land?"

Torbot McBlane threw her a sharp glance.

"Why should you think that?"

"It is just an idea that came to me."

She knew he debated with himself before he answered her question.

"It is true we have heard stories of hostile acts against other Clansmen who live near us, and although it is difficult to prove that it is Euan McBlane who is responsible for them, we have our suspicions."

"And have you tried to stop him from doing such things?"

Again she was aware that Torbot McBlane debated with himself whether he should tell her what was in his mind, and finally he said:

"He has a band of young men who follow him because they have nothing better to do."

"What you are saying is that he 'runs' a gang!"

Torbot McBlane nodded as if he could not bring himself to speak of it, and she asked sharply:

"Such behaviour must be stopped! I cannot allow the McBlanes to have a reputation for behaving in any way but what is correct and right for themselves and for their country."

Now Torbot McBlane was staring at her in surprise.

"You are speaking like your father," he said, "and those who are awaiting you will be proud to hear it."

"Why did Papa not speak to Euan if he knew what was going on?"

"As I have already said, My Lady, there is no real evidence against him. We only know, as the complaints pour in, that somebody is carrying on the feuds which are doing unprovoked harm to people who are struggling, just as our people are, to keep alive in the face of terrible difficulties."

"Then something must be done!" Clova declared. "I hope, Mr. McBlane, you will help me and guide me as you have done on this journey. If I am to be at all effective as your Chieftain, I must know the truth, the whole truth, and nothing must be kept from me. Do you understand?"

He nodded his head, and Clova said:

"Thank you! Thank you for being so kind to me, and for making me less afraid than I would otherwise have been to face what lies ahead of me."

She knew by the expression on his face that he was extremely gratified by what she had said.

She told herself that if she were honest, it was not only Torbot McBlane who had helped her, but also the Laird of Kilcowan, a man who, despite any attempts to stop her, she would see again, and not only see him, but help him.

* * *

When Clova had greeted those who had waited for her outside the front-door of the Castle, she found standing on the steps in the doorway a number of her relatives.

Most of them were elderly men, who looked in their kilts very much as her grandfather had looked, and who she gathered had known her as a child, although she could not remember them.

When she moved into the hall to climb the stairs up to the First Floor, where the main Reception Room was situated, there was one man standing a little back from the rest.

He came towards her with an expression in his eyes which made her know who he was before they were introduced.

"I do not suppose you remember your Cousin Euan McBlane?" one of the older men said.

"I am afraid not," Clova replied.

Then as she held out her hand and Euan took it, she had the feeling she was touching something poisonous and unclean.

It was not only the way he looked at her which made her shrink from the expression in his eyes, but it was something evil, or perhaps it was sheer hatred, that vibrated from him.

Instinctively, she took her hand from his more quickly that she should have done.

"It is a great pleasure to meet you, Cousin Clova."

His voice, she thought, was as unpleasant as he was himself.

"It is a great pleasure to be back," she answered firmly.

She thought his eyes narrowed as he asked:

"And do you really intend to stay?"

"Of course! This is where I belong!"

She spoke lightly, but she knew that those who heard what she said approved, while she was aware that Euan's thin lips tightened for a moment.

She turned away from him and started to climb the stairs, her relatives following her as she walked through the open doors of the Chieftain's Room.

It was a large, impressive room with long, high windows overlooking the gardens which led down to a small loch.

On the other side of it there was a woodland, and above them a steep hill so rocky that she remembered now it was never purple with heather like the rest of the moors.

She stood for a moment looking out of one of the windows. Then she realized that drinks were being poured out for the assembled guests, so that they could drink her health.

They toasted her in Gaelic, and then in English, as if to make sure she understood that they were welcoming her.

She thanked them, and as she spoke first to one, then to another, she was sure that Euan, who was somehow detached from the rest of the Clan, was watching her every move and doubtless listening to everything she said.

It made her feel almost as if he were waiting to pounce on her, and perhaps when no-one was watching, to assassinate her.

Then she told herself she was being ridiculous.

She refused to be intimidated by a young man who could not be older than twenty-eight or thirty, and who was already under suspicion of behaving badly by the Elders of the Clan.

Torbot McBlane had not joined the party, and she understood without being told that she would meet him again tomorrow when she received the Clan itself, and of course the Elders.

Now there were just her close relatives, and she learnt they were all staying in the Castle and tonight there would be a family dinner.

As they ate they would get to know their new Chieftain who had been taken away by her mother when she left secretly in the middle of the night.

It caused a scandal which would never be forgotten and would doubtless be written into the history of the McBlanes, just as their feuds and their victories had been.

But for the moment they talked to Clova only of her father, and how it had been a great tragedy when he had died of a heart-attack after over-exerting himself far too strenuously on a deer stalk which had taken over five hours.

"He was a fine sportsman," one of the older men in the party said, shaking his head. "But Alister would never listen to reason where his health was concerned."

"He got his stag before he died!" another member of the party said. "Quite frankly, that is the way I would like to die myself, either when I had just finished a stalk, or when I had bagged a brace of grouse!"

"And a terrible nuisance it would be to have to carry you down from the moor," another relative remarked jokingly. "So before you attempt to do anything so dramatic, I suggest you lose weight!"

There was laughter at this, and Clova knew that she liked her relatives.

At any rate, the gentlemen, with their talk about sport, and the way they looked at her with an unmistakable glint of admiration in their eyes.

This she could not fail to recognize, having for so many years seen exactly the same expression in the eyes of the men who looked at her mother when they first met her.

The women were more difficult, and she knew they were not looking at her face, but at her clothes.

She had chosen the plainest gown in which to travel, but although it was a very soft, unobtrusive shade of blue, it threw into prominence the perfection of her skin and the gold of her hair.

It was cut with the chic and brilliance of a French Couturier, who invariably accentuated the curves of a woman's body, the smallness of her waist, and the lissomness of her figure.

"I am afraid, Marchioness, you will find Scotland very dull after the gaieties of Paris," one of the elderly matrons said in a tone of voice which insinuated that Clova had indulged in all the wildest dissipations of the French Capital.

For a moment Clova thought of telling her how poor and even hungry she and her mother had been all the last year, and how their only dissipation had been to look in the shop windows at things they could not afford to buy.

Then she knew it would give them intense satisfaction to know that Lottie had suffered as they had hoped she would.

Also, undoubtedly, although they would rather die than admit it, they had envied her because they thought she was enjoying the forbidden fruits which they could never steal.

"I promise you," Clova said in her soft voice, "that I am now much enjoying being back in Scotland, and finding I remember far more things than I thought possible because I was so young when I left."

"I expect you will soon be longing for all the excitements you have missed," a woman said sourly.

"I doubt it," Clova replied. "I am sure I shall be too busy discovering all the things I have to do here to find time lying heavy on my hands."

"And what do you intend to do?" one of the gentlemen asked who had come up behind her as she was speaking.

"I intend," Clova said in a voice that seemed to ring out in the room, "to be not only a good and just, but an enlightened Chieftain."

There was a sudden silence before somebody asked the obvious question:

"What do you mean by 'enlightened'?"

"I mean," Clova replied, "that I want the Clan to embrace new ideas, to find new ways of gaining prosperity and, most of all, which I consider very important, I want peace."

As she spoke, she looked across the room, and as she met her Cousin Euan's eyes she knew by the sarcastic, cynical expression in his that they had declared war.

chapter four

BRAVE words, Clova thought to herself as she lay awake in the darkness, but they were useless unless they could be supported by action.

The difficulty was that she realised how ignorant she was not only of Scotland itself, but also of how she could actually help the Clansmen.

She found herself tossing and turning and wondering who would advise her, who would understand the difficulties.

At the same time, she knew the answer all too clearly: the one person she wanted to talk to was the Laird of Cowan.

"I must see him, I must!" she decided just before the first fingers of dawn showed in the sky.

Then at last, as if she had solved the problem for herself, she fell asleep.

She was awakened by her maid, Jeanne, who

looked after her, coming into the room and pulling back the curtains.

Because she had been so bewildered by everything last night, it was only now that Clova realised she was sleeping in the Chieftain's Room.

There was no mistaking it because she remembered being brought here when her grandfather was ill and thinking how impressive and frightening he looked propped up against a large number of pillows in the huge, carved oak four-poster.

She saw that one side of the great room was pierced by tall but narrow windows which told her they were part of one of the turrets, and on another wall stood a huge fireplace carved with the crest of the McBlanes.

There were several portraits, as she had already seen in other parts of the Castle, of her ancestors wearing their Chieftain's sporran and plaid clasped with a cairngorm brooch.

She thought as she lay in bed that they looked at her not exactly with disapproval, but as if there were a question in their eyes as to whether she was capable of following in their footsteps.

Now the fears of the night flooded over her again.

She felt so helpless and ineffective that it seemed the best thing she could do was to go back to France and make a life for herself there.

Then she remembered the bitterness in the Laird of Cowan's voice when he had spoken of his dead ewes, and told herself that if she did nothing else, she must stop her Cousin Euan from insulting and harassing another Clan.

By the time Clova was dressed, she felt a new strength in herself that had not been there previously.

As Jeanne buttoned up the plain but well-cut gown she was wearing of deep blue, which echoed the blue stripe in the McBlane tartan, the maid said:

"If Yer Ladyship looks outa the window, ye'll see the Clansmen gatherin'. They've come frae far an' near, an' I hear Yer Ladyship will be feastin' them, which be kind of ye, as many o' them have walked a lang way."

If that was what she was going to do, it was news to Clova, but she was sure her relatives, especially the older members, would see that she made no mistakes.

Only when she went into the Breakfast Room, where quite a number of guests in the Castle were already gathered, did she sense immediately that something had happened.

It seemed extraordinary, but their whole attitude towards her seemed to have changed, and for a moment she could not understand why it was so different or why she was so conscious of it.

Then when her Cousin Euan came into the room she understood.

He walked up to where she was sitting at the top of the table and said in an oily voice:

"Good morning, Cousin Clova! There is no need for me to tell you that you look very beautiful, and will doubtless fascinate and beguile our clansmen, just as we have all been captivated by our new Chieftain."

He looked round at the other relatives sitting at the table as he spoke, and as they obviously approved of what he said, Clova understood what had happened.

Last night they had accepted her and been polite to her for her father's sake and because she was by tonight to take his place.

But they still had reservations because of her mother, and because she had lived so many years in a foreign country.

Now she was sure that today they accepted her wholeheartedly and with enthusiasm because they had learnt that she was rich.

She knew that the only person who could have told them this was Torbot McBlane.

She guessed that after she had gone to bed early because she was so tired he must have come to the Castle and informed her older relatives of what he had learnt from *Monsieur* Beauvais in Paris.

They were now taking a very different view of her and she was quite certain from the expression on Euan's face that he was all the more determined to make her, as the Laird of Cowan had told her, his wife.

Clova felt herself tremble at the thought of it.

At the same time, because she could feel the approval of all her relatives vibrating towards her, she knew she was now in a position of authority that had not been possible yesterday.

It was degrading to think that she was not entirely accepted for herself!

Yet if her money could buy what she wanted for the Clan, and that more than anything else was peace, then she was prepared to forget her own feelings and accept her good fortune in the same way as her mother had done.

It seemed in a way ironic that her mother, who had been considered beneath contempt by the McBlanes, should be the instrument of bringing prosperity to the whole Clan.

Clova could almost hear her spontaneous and lilting laughter at the idea and she was certain that Lottie, if she knew of it, would think the whole thing a huge joke.

Because she wanted to make sure her surmise was correct, she asked the relative sitting next to her at the breakfast table, Sir Robert McBlane, an elderly, retired General, if he had met Torbot McBlane.

"I have known Torbot for forty years," he answered, "and I was saying to him last night that he was the right man to bring you home to your own land. I am sure he told you more eloquently than any of us could have done of the crisis Scotland is in at the moment, and how much help we need in the Highlands."

Clova knew from this that what she had thought was correct, and it was Torbot who had given her relatives the welcome information of how rich she was.

Euan had seated himself on her other side, and now he said:

"You must not be nervous of dealing with what lies in front of you, and, of course, I will be here to help you."

There was a possessive note in his voice that made her say a little stiffly:

"Thank you, Cousin Euan, it is very kind of you to offer to help me, but I think I shall turn for advice to Sir Robert, who, I suspect, is the oldest of my relatives."

The General was obviously very gratified.

"I will look after you, my child," he said. "I was beside your father when he greeted the Clansmen after your grandfather's death, and a very fine speech he made! They have never forgotten it."

"So I am expected to speak!" Clova exclaimed.

"If it is something you are not used to," Euan said quickly, "let me do it for you."

There was an eagerness in his voice which told her he was longing to assert his authority and make the Clansmen realise how important he was.

"I am perfectly willing to speak," Clova answered, "and I know exactly what I want to say to those who have come so far to meet me."

She knew Euan was annoyed that she did not accept his offer, but the General said:

"Of course you must speak! It is traditional for the Chieftain to greet the Clansmen and to tell them they can turn to him for help when they need it."

Clova smiled at him, and he said comfortingly:

"Now, do not worry, dear. They will offer you their obeisance, and all you have to do is to say something to each one of them which they will cherish as if it were a rare jewel."

Clova thought he was quite poetical, and she thanked him again, adding:

"I understand from my maid that we provide them with food and, perhaps, drink."

The General looked embarrassed.

"It was not until last night when I was talking to Torbot that we understood it was something you could afford. As I could not ask your permission so late in the evening, I have ordered on your behalf two oxen to be slaughtered, and for barrels of ale to be provided. That is something the Clansmen will appreciate and remember for years."

"I am glad you did that," Clova said simply.

When breakfast was over, the General's wife and

two of the other ladies draped a plaid over Clova's left shoulder and fastened it with the huge cairngorm brooch that her father had worn.

It was something she had not expected to wear.

She could not help thinking it must have been her Celtic blood which had made her choose for her gown exactly the right shade of blue which went with the McBlane tartan.

She was also surprised when they produced a tartan bonnet which they told her had been worn many years ago by her great-grandmother when, during her husband's absence at the wars, she had taken his place at some of the gatherings of the Clan.

It was small and neatly made, and when she looked at herself in the mirror, Clova thought it was exceedingly becoming.

She had in fact been a little worried in case the fashionable head gear she had bought in Paris to go with her gown would seem inappropriate for such an occasion.

But now with her plaid and her tartan bonnet she knew she looked exactly as a woman who was so fortunate as to take a man's place as the Chieftain of the Clan should look.

When she went downstairs she found all her relatives waiting for her in the hall. Euan at once put out his hand towards her, but she moved quickly to the General's side and took his arm.

"You look very nice, my dear," he said.

Knowing he was trying to give her courage, she thanked him, and she was sure that he had sensed that she was avoiding Euan.

The servants opened the great oak door, and as they did so the pipers outside started to play "Call of

73

the McBlanes," and the sound was taken up by a dozen other pipers scattered over the ground in front of the Castle.

Clova thought she would never forget the picture the Clansmen made as they stood waiting for her below a mound of green grass on which there had been set the Chieftain's chair made from the horns of stags.

There were no other seats, and as the pipers marched ahead, the General escorted Clova to it and she sat down in the chair that had been occupied by her ancestors for centuries.

Her male relatives, looking resplendent in their kilts and sporrans, stood behind her.

Then, one by one, the Clansmen came up, dropped down on one knee in front of her, and taking her hand swore allegiance to her as their Chieftain.

She found it very moving as each man said his name clearly and without mumbling, and swore that he would serve her until he died.

The General knew most of the men and what their occupation was.

If he faltered, another relative, almost as old as he was, standing on the other side of her supplied her with the information that the man kneeling at her feet was a shepherd or a farmer, a river watcher, a ghillie, or a stalker.

There were more shepherds than anything else, and Clova had already learnt from Torbot McBlane that the land she owned was better for sheep than that of many of their neighbours.

There were perhaps nearly three hundred Clansmen present at the ceremony, but Clova could remember Torbot McBlane telling her that before the

Clearances there had been nearly two thousand.

"Now the McBlanes are scattered all over the world," he said sadly, "but those who keep in touch with their Clansmen at home will learn they have a new Chieftain."

Clova found it hard to think that any of the McBlanes who had been forced to leave Scotland for Canada or other distant lands, or their descendants, would still be interested in what happened at home.

Then she remembered that the Scots never forget, and knew that Torbot was right and they would want to know exactly what was happening.

What she found very touching was that many of the Clansmen brought with them small gifts which she accepted, then handed to the General to place on one side.

There were gloves they had knitted from the wool of their sheep which they had spun on a wheel and then dyed in various colours; there were scarves which their wives had woven on hand-looms at home.

There was a grouse's claw preserved and fashioned as a brooch, a clump of black-cock feathers for a bonnet, and from those who lived near the sea there were little shell-covered boxes.

Clova thanked them profusely in her soft voice, and told the giver how grateful she was for such a charming gift and that it was something she would always treasure.

She knew how gratified they were.

Then when the last Clansman had made his obeisance as she rose to her feet she found herself thinking of the Laird of Cowan.

It was almost as if he were there beside her,

prompting her, so that she did not have to think of what she should say, and the words came to her lips.

She heard her voice ringing out so that all the Clansmen, now sitting as they had been told to do, could hear her.

Their worried eyes, their long ragged hair and weather-beaten skin, made her feel that she wanted, more than she had ever wanted anything in her life, to help and protect them.

She did not miss that many of them were wearing kilts that were torn and threadbare and boots that were so dilapidated that it must have been agony to walk in them for any distance.

She thought, too, that some of them looked as if they did not have enough to eat, and she knew from her own experience what that meant and how difficult they must find it to keep going when their stomachs were empty.

First she greeted them and told them how glad she was to be back in the home of her ancestors, and how, even though she had been away for so long, she was finding everything so familiar that she was beginning to feel as if she had never left.

They cheered at this, and she went on to say what an honour and a privilege it was to take the place of her grandfather, whom she remembered well, and of her father, whom she knew they had admired and respected.

"It is going to be difficult, because I am a woman," she said, "to take his place or be as good a Chieftain as he was, but I feel sure that with your help I can do it. But never forget that I need you as much as you need me!"

She paused and then went on.

"I want you to come to me with your troubles, just as I am willing to consult you about mine, and if we work together, I am sure that we can make our Clan more distinguished than it is already, and set an example to all other Clans, some of which I understand are vitally in need of it."

This made the men laugh and she went on.

"Because I am young, I want to bring you new ideas and to sweep away some of the older ones which are out of date. The first thing which is important is that we should try to make ourselves more prosperous and make certain that no one with the name of McBlane is actually suffering from any form of privation!"

She paused, then as she glanced round at the presents she had been given which had been laid by the General on one side of her chair, she had a sudden idea.

"When I was in Edinburgh on my journey here," she said, "I saw in the Hotel in which I stayed a number of articles for sale set out to attract the tourists. There were scarves, gloves, and other things rather similar to these you have brought me.

"But I suspect, although they were labelled as made in Scotland, many of them come from England, or perhaps from the British Colonies Overseas."

She knew the men were listening intently and continued.

"I am determined that we should make sure that the tourists who come to Scotland shall buy and take away with them things that really have been made in our country. That is why I am going to suggest to you that, as your wives have made these delightful gifts for me, they should make many more which can be sold.

"I will personally see if there are any shops in Edinburgh, Glasgow, or other towns in Scotland which will take what we have to sell, so that you will benefit from everything you produce."

She threw out her hands and added:

"There is one way by which we could establish a small Highland industry in our own cottages and on our own land and make it profitable."

She heard her relatives mutter behind her but went on.

"And because I think it could be a very good way of not only helping ourselves, but of publicising the ingenuity of Scottish minds, I intend to find a cottage fairly near the Castle where we can not only display everything that you make, but also sell the goods so that you yourselves can see what interests the buyers and what attracts them as a souvenir of the Highlands."

There was a startled gasp as she paused, then a burst of applause.

When it died down Clova went on:

"There is just one more thing I have to say to you, but it is very important: if we are to move together, and I mean together, into a new era for ourselves and the country we love so much, we must sweep away the ugly and bitter feuds which have existed for many years between many of the Clans, but are now out of date, ridiculous, and harmful to our progress."

She did not turn her head but she was sure Euan was scowling.

"What we have to concern ourselves with," she continued, "is the real enemies of this country, which are poverty, ignorance, and indolence. Those are the evils which sap the strength of our people and which are completely alien to the real Scot who has survived through wars and pestilence, injustice, and at times unbelievable cruelty."

Her voice rose.

"But we have survived, and now having fought through the darkness, we could enter into the sunshine of a very different and very much happier life."

She paused.

"So I beg of you to throw away anything that is not constructive to the future, anything which will not benefit your children, and unite with every other Scot, whatever Clan he comes from, remembering only that his blood is the same as ours, and that if we really try, we can make Scotland great, and indeed far greater than it has ever been in the past!"

She sat down and for a moment there was a silence which every orator knows is the greatest compliment he can possibly receive.

Then the Clan were on their feet, cheering wildly, flinging their bonnets in the air, their voices ringing out, until it seemed the whole Strath was echoing back their enthusiasm.

It was so spontaneous and so moving that Clova felt the tears coming into her eyes, and she heard Sir Robert say very quietly:

"Well done!"

She knew, too, that her other relatives were all clapping.

At the same time, a sneaking glance at Euan told her that although he was clapping automatically, there was a twist to his thin lips and an expression in his eyes which she did not want to translate.

Afterwards they went back into the Castle while the Clansmen started to carve up the oxen which had been roasting at one side of the ground.

Servants were bringing out barrels of ale, while the Elders, and there were six of them, headed by Torbot McBlane, came into the Castle to drink Clova's health in whisky.

Because she valued his approval more than anyone else's, Clova went up to him, and as he took her hand he said:

"I was very proud of you, My Lady."

"I hoped that was what you would say," Clova replied, "and so you think my idea of establishing our own small Highland industry a good one?"

"Very good," he agreed, "if it is possible."

"We have to make it possible," Clova said. "I am sure there is somebody you can recommend who would go to Edinburgh and Glasgow to find out which shops would be interested in taking what we can produce."

"There are certainly shops that could take them, if they cared," Torbot McBlane said.

"Then we will have to make them care," Clova said firmly.

He looked at her with approval, then Euan was beside her saying:

"An excellent speech, my dear Cousin! I am beginning to think that while you were living in France you must have taken the stage at some time, or else you were on a political platform."

"Neither!" Clova replied. "But I have listened to a large number of eloquent speakers, and I always hoped that if the day came when I had to make a speech, I would not fail to hold my audience."

"There is no doubt you did that," he said, "but I wondered what you meant by your reference to feuds. Surely you cannot believe they still exist in our part of the world?"

He looked her straight in the eye as he spoke, and she thought he was not so much trying to convince her by what he was saying as hoping to find out how much she knew.

She did not reply, however, and after a moment he said:

"I was told, although it may have been just a rumour, that on your way here yesterday you talked with a stranger on the banks of the River Suisgill."

Clova raised her eyebrows.

"Is that what the river is called? It certainly had some fine salmon in it!"

"And who was the fisherman to whom you were talking?" Euan enquired.

"A Scotsman." Clova smiled.

She moved away as she spoke to address one of the Elders who was in attendance at the Castle.

He was obviously eager to talk to her and embarked on a long and rather boring discourse on the difficulties they had encountered the previous Winter, when the snow had been so deep.

Clova found it hard to listen because she was wondering who could have informed Euan of what she had done yesterday, and whether he realised that the fisherman whom she had helped land the salmon was the Laird of Cowan.

She felt his informant might have been the coachman, but then she remembered there were always stalkers on the moors in Scotland, watching not only the stags, but the movements and behaviour of human beings.

It made her more determined than ever to see the Laird of Cowan again, but she was far from certain how it would be possible for her to do so.

Fortunately all her relatives were so agreeable and so pleasant, now that they knew how rich she was, that it was easy during the afternoon to suggest to an unmarried Cousin, whose name was Jamie McBlane, that she would like to go riding.

He was a man of about forty and she had heard somebody say that his sole interest was horses.

The moment she mentioned it, his eyes seemed to light up, and she knew he was interested.

"I have not ridden for some years," she said, "but I wondered if it would be possible for you to find a horse for me to ride tomorrow morning. I would like to see something of the land around the Castle, and perhaps you would ride with me?"

"Nothing could give me greater pleasure!" he replied.

Clova hesitated, then she said:

"I think it would be more pleasant if we could ride alone. If a lot of people were watching me, I would feel embarrassed."

He laughed.

"I know exactly what you are feeling, and if you are able to get up as early as seven o'clock, then we will ride before breakfast."

"I would love that," Clova said, and gave him a conspiratorial smile before she moved away.

What she wanted to discover was how to reach Cowan Castle in the shortest possible time.

She had the idea that to follow the road she had come by, winding up the hills and down until it finally reached the McBlane Castle, would be a longer way round than was necessary, but she knew it would be a mistake to ask questions.

The day passed with the Elders holding what Clova felt was a planned series of meetings with her, and escorting her amongst the Clansmen as they enjoyed themselves after eating and drinking.

Some could not stay long because they had to be back with their flocks, and Clova learnt that there were many who were unable to be present because they had no one to leave in charge of their sheep or cattle.

"If a man has a young wife without too many small children, he can usually ask her to take his place for a short time," Torbot McBlane explained, "but otherwise it is impossible. Besides, the distances are very great."

"I understand," Clova said, "but I would like sometime to visit those who live a long way from the Castle and who would therefore not have a chance of meeting me."

She knew this gained his approval, and after the Elders had said their farewells and only a few Clansmen were left celebrating outside the Castle, Clova felt she must rest for a little while.

She was just going to her bedroom when she thought she would take a newspaper or perhaps a book to read from the Library, which was situated next to the Chieftain's Room.

She entered it and had not been looking round for more than a few seconds, when the door opened and Euan came in.

She had, although it annoyed her, been acutely aware of him all day, and while she had tried to forget him, she was always conscious of the fact that he was not far from her, watching her with his dark eyes.

Now, as she stood in front of one of the bookcases, he walked to her side and said:

"At last I have a chance to tell you how well you have done, and how completely you have captivated the hearts of our people."

"Thank you," Clova said, and added quickly: "But I am a little tired and am eager to take the opportunity of lying down for a rest before dinner."

As she spoke she was very conscious that Euan was standing nearer to her than was necessary, and although she did not look at him directly, she knew that his eyes were on her face.

"I wanted to add," he said in a low voice, "that you have also captivated me!"

Clova managed a light laugh.

"I doubt if that is true, Cousin Euan," she smiled, "but if it is, I have a feeling you had very different ideas about me last night."

"Why should you think that?" he enquired.

"Perhaps it is my Celtic blood which makes me perceptive," she answered, "or perhaps I am sensible enough to realise that you would have preferred the Chieftain of the McBlanes to be a man, and why not yourself?"

As she spoke she was making sure she struck first, and she hoped she had disconcerted him.

"There is one very easy way to satisfy my ambition, if that is what it is," Euan said.

With what was a good attempt at acting, Clova put up her hand to her lips as if to stifle a yawn.

"You must forgive me," she said, "but I really feel quite exhausted and I wish to rest."

"I will not keep you long," Euan replied, "but I insist that you hear me out."

"Insist?" Clova questioned sharply.

Then as she looked at him she saw by the expression on his face that he was determined not to let her escape.

She felt a streak of fear, and turning away she took at random a book from one of the shelves.

"What I have to say to you," Euan said, "is quite simply that I want you to marry me!"

Clova was still for a moment.

Then with a well-simulated expression of surprise she turned round.

"Did you really ask me, Cousin Euan, to... marry you?"

"I intend to marry you, and that will make everything, as you must see, very simple. I can help you to make the Clan more important, as you wish to do, and we will also manage to enjoy ourselves."

"You make it sound very... attractive," Clova replied, trying not to sound sarcastic, "but you will appreciate that I met you for the first time last night. I know nothing about you, and while of course I am honoured by your suggestion, it is... something I could not possibly... answer until we knew each other... better."

"I know everything about you I need to know," Euan said, "and if like all women, you are craving for love, then I can promise you it is something which will not be missing in our marriage."

He would have put his arms round her, but Clova stepped away from him.

"It is far too soon even to... think of... such a thing!" she cried. "And as I have already told you ...I am too... tired to talk... or do anything... except sleep."

She would have walked to the door, but Euan was in front of her and stood blocking the way.

"You may think it is easy to evade me," he said, "but I know that I want not only to marry you, but also to make love to you. You are very attractive, my little cousin from France, and I dare say your French education in the joys and splendour of love will do a great deal to enlighten the Scottish scene."

Clova felt there was a coarse innuendo behind what he was saying, and it was as if he were mocking at her for being prudish, when her mother had been Lottie.

"I do not know what you... mean," she said, "but thank you, Cousin Euan, for asking me to be your wife. However, as I have already said, it is a question I shall be unable to answer until I know you as a man, and as somebody I could respect and honour as... my husband."

To her consternation Euan put out his hands to hold her by the shoulders.

"You are being very evasive!" he said harshly. "Are you telling me that young though you are, there is already a man in your life? What were you doing, you and your flighty mother, all the time you were in Paris?"

He shook her slightly before he went on.

"I am a man of the world, and I am not taken in

by that young and innocent air. You are old enough and woman enough to want a man, and you will find it incredibly dull here without one."

As he spoke, Clova could feel his fingers biting into the softness of her skin, and she felt, too, that his face was drawing nearer and nearer to hers. He was evil, and she knew he was dangerous and menacing.

Her heart was beating with fear and her lips were dry.

Then with a sudden movement which took him by surprise she shook herself free of him, saying:

"Leave me... alone! You have no... right to... speak to me like... that!"

He would have caught hold of her again, and she was wondering frantically how she could escape from him when the door opened, and to her utter relief the General entered.

He was accompanied by another elderly man, and they both had cigars between their lips and were obviously looking for somewhere to sit quietly, where they would not be disturbed.

Without speaking, Clova slipped hastily past them before Euan could prevent her from doing so.

Then because she was frightened, she was running as quickly as she could down the corridor towards her own bedroom.

Only when she reached it was she aware that her heart was beating frantically in her breast and she realized how frightened she was of Euan, who was positively menacing.

Something told her it would be hard to escape not only from his attentions, but also from him personally and physically.

"I hate him!" she told herself.

She knew that he was evil and he would persist in his pursuit of her, not only because he wanted to share the Chieftainship with her, in the position of her husband, but also because he desired her money.

She sat down on the side of the bed and suddenly felt very young and helpless.

This was the sort of difficulty she had not expected in Scotland of all places.

She had thought that after all she had seen of her mother's life she should be able to handle men.

She should certainly not allow herself to be scared by a ne'er-do-well like her cousin.

Yet there was something about him which was different from any of the men she had ever met with Lottie, although there was no doubt that many of them had been flashy, suave, and lustful.

She could remember noticing the fire in their eyes when they looked at her mother and the deep note of desire in their voices when they spoke to her.

But it was very different from the way Euan had spoken to her and she knew that he wanted her not only as a man wants a woman, which she could understand and cope with, but as a symbol of his ambitions and a source of wealth.

'If I...married him...I am sure he...would kill me,' she thought.

Then she told herself she was being over-dramatic, but at the same time, she could not suppress the thought and it made her tremble.

"I must talk to...somebody. I must see... somebody who will...understand and who will tell me what to...do!"

Then she remembered that tomorrow when she went riding with Jamie she would make sure she found out the way to Castle Cowan.

After that she could decide how best to reach its Laird.

chapter five

RIDING out of the stableyard with Jamie McBlane, Clova was conscious of feeling wildly excited.

She was thrilled by the beauty of the morning sunshine percolating through the trees, the mist over the moors, and the glimmer of silver when she was within sight of the river.

It was all so lovely, so very unlike France, and she found herself exulting:

'This is mine—mine!'

She rode South from the Castle, deliberately keeping below the road which began to rise almost immediately over the moors.

They moved slowly along the river, where it was easy going for the horses, and a number of sheep were grazing on the green grass.

Clova found it thrilling to be once again on horseback, although she was certain that after years of not riding she would later be very stiff.

When her mother had first run away from Scotland with Lionel Arkwright, she had ridden every day with them both in the Bois.

Even after he had left them, there were several of Lottie's admirers who owned outstanding stables, and because Clova was a very pretty child they had enjoyed taking her riding with them.

It was only later, when Lottie's suitors were apt to belong to other social circles and some of them, like Jan Maskill, came from far-off countries, that there were no horses for Clova to ride.

But the last three years had been barren of horseflesh, and Clova now felt an irrepressible joy and excitement because she was riding again and her horse was well-bred and spirited.

She had seen in the stables and in the Park round the Castle sturdy little ponies used on the moors, and she looked forward to riding them.

At the moment, however, she was concerned more than anything else to discover where Castle Cowan was situated.

It seemed to her that they very quickly reached the place near the river where she had helped Tarquil Cowan land his salmon.

It was then she had an idea, but was half-afraid to express it.

She had found out that her Cousin Jamie had an estate of his own which, she gathered from what he had said, was prosperous.

As they talked she found that although he was not very eloquent, he was very interested in current affairs.

She was sure he was in fact more enlightened than

some of her other relatives.

They had ridden quite a way before he said:

"I think now, Cousin Clova, we have reached the boundary of the McBlane estate in this direction. It extends very much farther North and also West, but here it is bordered by the land belonging to the McCowans."

Clova drew in her breath, then she said:

"You heard what I said yesterday, Cousin Jamie, about repudiating the ancient feuds."

"I thought you were quite right," he said.

She smiled at him, then she asked:

"In that case, are you brave enough to come with me to call on the Laird of Cowan?"

There was a little pause when her Cousin did not reply. Then he asked:

"Do you know the Laird?"

"I met him on my way to Strathblane."

"And he seemed friendly—not hostile in any way?"

"Not in the least," Clova replied, "although he has suffered severely from the way some of the McBlanes are treating him."

She knew by the expression in Jamie's eyes that he was aware of what had occurred, and that he had been told that Euan was suspected of harassing the McCowans.

There was a pause as she waited, holding her breath until Jamie McBlane said slowly:

"I am quite happy to accompany you to Castle Cowan, if that is what you wish."

"Thank you," Clova said. "I knew that you would not be so hidebound and so out of date as to wish to carry on this absurd enmity towards a neighbour."

They rode over the border following the river and after a little while Jamie said hastily:

"I am afraid that you will find it difficult to convince some of our relatives that what you are doing is the right thing."

"Then there is no need to tell them," Clova said, "except that I expect they will learn about it sooner or later. I am beginning to think that in Scotland even the sheep talk and the heather itself has ears!"

Jamie laughed.

"There is very little that can be kept hidden."

"I am aware of that, and if they are disagreeable about what we are doing, I shall look to you to support me," Clova said.

They rode on and ten minutes later could see the Castle ahead of them.

As she drew nearer she realised the Laird had been right in saying it was in a dilapidated state.

It was very old, only one tower was still intact, and the battlements were in need of repair.

At the same time, there was a small Loch in front of it which stretched from the head of the river, and with the moors stretching out behind it, was so lovely that Clova drew in her breath.

For a moment it seemed almost to have a fairylike quality about it, and she was afraid it might vanish before she reached it.

But it was still there as they rode up to the door and a number of sporting-dogs came running out towards them, not barking or aggressive, but wagging their tails as if in welcome.

Jamie dismounted and Clova held the bridle of his horse as he pulled at an iron bell that hung beside an oak door studded and with iron hinges.

They waited for some time before the door was opened not by a servant, but by the Laird of Cowan himself.

For a moment he looked first at Jamie, then at Clova in surprise.

"Good morning!" Jamie said. "Our new Chieftain, the Marchioness of Strathblane, was eager to call on you, and I escorted her."

"I am delighted to see you," the Laird said, holding out his hand.

Then he walked towards Clova to stare up at her as she sat looking exceedingly elegant in a green habit she had bought in Paris.

Their eyes met and she knew without his saying so how glad he was to see her.

"It is very courteous of you to visit me," he said aloud. "May I invite you in for breakfast. I was just about to have my own."

"We would be delighted!" Clova answered.

The servant who had followed the Laird out of the house now took the reins of the two horses, and Tarquil Cowan reached up to lift Clova from the saddle.

As he did so she was for a moment in his arms and she felt a little sensation she had never felt before.

It seemed somehow to tingle in her breasts and move from there up to her lips before he released her.

In a voice that only she could hear he said:

"I have been praying that I would see you again."

She felt the colour come into her cheeks and her eyes fell before his.

Then with an effort she walked ahead of him up the steps and in through the front door.

It was impossible not to compare the interior of

Tarquil Cowan's Castle with her own.

It was smaller, but the rooms were well-proportioned, and the view from the windows was exquisite.

The floors were bare except for a few fur or skin rugs made from stags or wild-cats and the walls were decorated mostly with stags' horns.

The curtains were threadbare and tattered and, although the chairs and sofas were comfortable, they were badly in need of recovering.

Tarquil Cowan took them through what Clova knew was the Chieftain's Room into the Dining-Room, which opened out of it.

Again the windows looked over the Loch and the moors beyond, and the fireplace was impressive.

There were rugs of the same type on the floor, and the table with its clean white cloth had none of the silver or the expensive porcelain that was used at Strathblane.

Nevertheless, when they were seated, a kilted servant brought first a fresh pot of coffee, then eggs and bacon, which had obviously been prepared quickly in the kitchen.

The bread was warm from the oven, but the butter was not of the same quality that Clova had eaten yesterday, and she guessed that Tarquil's cattle did not give as good milk as those which now belonged to her.

She was, however, not disposed to be critical, being so excited to have reached Castle Cowan and to see the man she had thought of incessantly ever since they had met.

As they started to eat Tarquil said:

"I have heard what you said in your speech yesterday, and I thought it was very brave of you, and even braver to come here today."

"You heard?" Clova exclaimed. "How could you have done?"

He smiled.

"Everything is known in Scotland almost as soon as it happens."

"That is just what I was saying to my Cousin Jamie as we rode here."

"As a matter of fact, it was particularly easy for me," Tarquil smiled, "because one of my herdsmen bravely married a McBlane, and her brother, with whom she is in constant touch, is one of your gillies."

Clova laughed, then she said:

"You see, Jamie? I was right, and I suspect even the fish are talking about what we do."

Clova looked at Tarquil and said:

"When I woke up this morning my first thought was that it was very easy to say what should be done, but very much more difficult to make sure that it is."

She could see by the expression on his face that he knew exactly what she was thinking, and he said quietly:

"There was another incident yesterday, when one of my shepherds saw a young man attempting to carry away two new-born lambs, and although they were shaken, they suffered no damage, and when they were returned to their mother they survived."

There was a note of anger in Tarquil's voice as he spoke that was unmistakable, and after a moment's embarrassed silence Jamie asked:

"Have you any idea who would do anything so disgraceful?"

"My shepherd was certain the man in question was wearing the kilt of the McBlanes."

"This sort of thing has got to stop!" Clova exclaimed. "You do not yet know, Jamie, but the Laird recently found two of his best ewes with their throats cut!"

"I agree it is disgraceful," Jamie said. "Perhaps, Cousin Clova, your Clan will listen to what you said yesterday and obey you."

"In the old days the Clansmen were punished for disobedience," Tarquil said, "but now it is much more difficult."

"Perhaps we shall be able to find out who was the instigator of such crimes," Clova said.

The two men to whom she was speaking were looking at her and she knew as she spoke that they were both aware that she was referring to her Cousin Euan.

Abandoning all pretence, Clova said:

"We must stop him!"

"I will try," Jamie said, "but it will be difficult unless we can catch him red-handed."

"Surely that could happen?" Clova asked.

"We are both thinking of the same person," Tarquil said. "But he is too clever actually to commit a crime himself. He merely gives orders to those who find it an adventure to follow him, and in my opinion are more sinned against than sinning."

Clova was sure this was true.

Euan was an educated, intelligent man with a sharp but twisted brain, and the youths he had recruited into his special gang were impressed by him, and he could manipulate them in any way he wished.

Once again Clova felt helpless, knowing that because she was a woman it would be harder to assert her authority than if she were a man.

As they rose from the breakfast-table, Tarquil making no apology for the fact that it was a frugal meal, Jamie said:

"I wonder if you would allow me to look at your tower, which I know is the oldest part of the Castle. I am, as it happens, extremely interested in the historical buildings of our country, many of which are being sadly neglected."

"Yes, of course," Tarquil replied.

He led the way to the end of the Castle, where there was door which led to the tower.

He opened it and Jamie started to climb the very narrow twisting stairway.

"It is quite safe," Tarquil said, "except that you have to be careful on top of the tower itself."

"I will take care," Jamie replied, who by now had turned the corner of the stairs and was out of sight.

Clova expected to follow him, but Tarquil blocked her way.

He stood looking at her and once again she felt shy, her eye-lashes dark against her cheeks.

"It was very wonderful of you," he said in a low voice, "to come to me like this. I have been wondering almost every minute since we met how I could see you again, but could not think of a way."

"You . . . wanted to see me?"

"I dare not tell you how much."

There was a little pause before Clova asked:

"Will you help me in what I am . . . trying to do?"

"I have already sworn my allegiance to you," Tarquil answered, "and you know I am yours to command."

He moved a step nearer to her and said in a very different tone of voice:

"But my dear, take care of yourself! I am afraid for you."

"I am... afraid... too," Clova said in a little more than a whisper.

"Of your Cousin Euan?"

"Yes."

"He has not threatened you?"

"No, but he has already asked me to... marry him, just as you... said he... might."

"He has not wasted much time," the Laird said, and she thought there was a bitter note in his voice.

There was a little silence, then he went on.

"I have been thinking that it is important you should make a Will leaving your money to anybody rather than your husband."

"Are you really... suggesting that I might... marry Cousin Euan?" Clova enquired.

"I am afraid he might trap you into becoming his wife. Remember, in Scotland we have the Law of Marriage by Consent."

"Yes, I know that," Clova answered, "but I would never, never consent to marry him, whatever he might say."

"He might make it impossible for you to refuse him."

"How could he do... that?"

She realised that Tarquil was finding it hard to think of the words in which to answer her.

Because she was afraid that Jamie would come back, and they would no longer be able to go on talking, she said:

"Help me, you must help me...I am afraid of him. Last night he said he intended to marry me, even though I told him it was far too soon to contemplate such a thing."

"I will try to protect you," Tarquil said, "but it will not be easy. Besides..."

His eyes met hers and his voice died away.

For a moment it seemed to Clova as if they met each other across time and space, and she knew he was the man she had dreamt of, the man she had always wanted to find but thought it impossible.

There was no need for words.

She knew by the expression in Tarquil's eyes, and the vibrations she could feel joining her to him so that neither of them could move, that he loved her as she loved him.

Then with what seemed an almost superhuman effort Tarquil turned away.

"I will try to protect you, if it is humanly possible," he said harshly, "but in the position I am in there is nothing else I can say."

He walked across to the window and stood with his back to her.

Clova knew he was thinking not only of her high rank as the Marchioness of Strathblane, but also of her money, while he was comparatively so poor.

She wanted to tell him that nothing mattered but what she felt pulsating through her body, running in her veins like shafts of sunshine.

Then as she hesitated because she was shy, she heard footsteps coming down from the tower and knew that Jamie was returning.

Tarquil heard them, too, and he turned round. As

they looked at each other and the expression in his eyes made Clova quiver, he said very quietly:

"Trust me!"

* * *

Riding home, Jamie talked enthusiastically about Cowan Castle and especially of the tower.

"It is one of the oldest I have ever seen," he said, "and I intend when I return to describe it to some of my friends in Stirling, who are all ardent archaeologists."

"How interesting," Clova said.

"They are not only writing a book about Scotland," he went on, "but are trying to raise funds to preserve some of the better examples of buildings erected by our forebears. I feel, as they do, that they are not only part of our history but of real value to the Scotsmen who will follow us in the future."

"I am so glad you feel like that," Clova said, "and it was very kind and helpful of you, Cousin Jamie, to visit the Laird with me."

"He is a very nice young man," Jamie replied. "It seems hard that he should be so impoverished that he cannot restore his Castle or improve his herds."

They were both of them aware as they rode home that the sheep grazing around Castle Cowan were inferior to those on the McBlane land, and what cattle could be seen were pitiable thin.

"If only I could help him!" Clova whispered to herself.

She found herself wishing that he was living in a Castle as grand and prosperous as Strathblane and that she was the poor "Cinderella" in Castle Cowan.

In that case things would be very much easier, for she had the frightening feeling that because Tarquil was proud—and what Scotsman was not?—he would erect a barrier between them, a barrier springing not from the feuds of the past, but from her wealth.

There was no need to ask herself if he knew about it.

She was quite certain that what Torbot had told her relatives was already common knowledge amongst the Clansmen, and the McCowan who was married to the sister of one of her gillies would have received the information and told his own Chieftain about it.

They reached Strathblane Castle and although it was nearly half after nine, Clova and Jamie went into the Breakfast-Room, where there was only the General and his wife still seated at the table.

Euan was just leaving the room as they entered it.

"Where have you been?" he asked furiously as Clova appeared.

"I have been riding with Cousin Jamie."

"I would have ridden with you if you had asked me."

"I was very happy to have Cousin Jamie's company," Clova replied, "and it has been delightful to have the chance of being on horseback again."

She knew Euan was angry, and she moved quickly to the head of the table and sat down.

"Good morning, Cousin Robert," she said to the General. "Good morning, Cousin Mary."

"I want to talk to you, Clova," Lady McBlane replied, "but I do not wish you to think that we are pushing or imposing upon you in any way."

"I would never think that," Clova smiled.

"In which case, my dear," Lady McBlane went on, "I am going to suggest that my husband and I should stay with you here at the Castle as chaperons until you find perhaps another relative you would rather have as a guest."

Clova gave a delighted cry.

"I would love you to do that!" she said. "How very kind of you to think of it!"

"Most of our other relations are leaving today," the General said, "and I do not like to think of you here alone, my dear."

"It is very kind of you," Clova replied, then was aware that Euan had come back to the table.

"I have already said that I shall be here," he said aggressively, "and my Factor's wife, who is an extremely nice woman, is prepared to move into the Castle if you are in need of a chaperon. She is young enough for you to find her a very charming companion."

He had it all thought out, Clova thought, and felt as if he were enclosing her in a prison from which she could not escape.

"It is kind of you to think of it, Cousin Euan," she said lightly, "but of course I would far rather have the General and Cousin Mary with me, as they have suggested. After all, they knew well both Papa and my grandfather and therefore nobody could advise me and help me better than they can."

She saw the expression of anger in Euan's face, and he gave an exclamation that was almost an oath as he walked out of the Breakfast-Room and slammed the door behind him.

"Insolent young puppy!"

The General spoke beneath his breath, but Clova heard him.

Impulsively she put her hand on his.

"Please stay with me, Cousin Robert," she pleaded.

There was a little tremor of fear in her voice which neither the General nor his wife missed.

"You are not to worry yourself," Lady McBlane said. "We thought it out very carefully before we suggested it, and we would like you to look on Robert as if he were your Guardian, and the father which, poor child, you have not had for so many years."

She gave a little sigh as she said:

"I think if you had known him when he grew older you would have loved Alister as we did, and when he became Chieftain, he was much more understanding and compassionate than he had ever been as a younger man."

"I wish I had known him then," Clova said. "But I feel sure that you will make up for what I missed, and also... protect me."

There was no need to explain from whom, for she saw the glance the General exchanged with his wife and knew they both disliked Euan, and perhaps like herself were a little afraid of him.

During the morning and immediately after luncheon most of the other guests from other parts of the estate left, driving away in their carriages, which had made quite a display in the stable-yard.

They all expressed their delight with their new Chieftain, and were obviously eager to be invited again to the Castle as soon as possible.

Only when after luncheon a number of them left at

the same time was Clova aware that Euan was assuming the position of host, and saying good-bye to them in very much the same way as she was.

There was nothing she could do to stop him, but she knew he was doing it deliberately to impress himself on her, and to make everybody else assume that it was only a question of time before they would enjoy his hospitality as her husband as well as hers.

'I hate him!' she thought.

As she waved to the last of the departing guests, Euan was standing beside her, too close and in too familiar an attitude, on the doorstep.

"I certainly think they enjoyed themselves!" he said in a possessive tone. "We must invite them again."

Clova felt her temper rising.

"This is my Castle," she said, "and I shall decide whom I ask, and when."

He laughed, and it was an unpleasant sound.

"I think you will find," he said, "that the McBlanes do what they wish, when they wish, and it is very difficult for anybody to circumvent them. That, my dear little Cousin Clova, applies also to me!"

"Then you are going to be disappointed," Clova retorted, and walked away from him up the steps.

"Will you come driving with me?" Euan asked as he followed her. "I would like to take you to a part of our land which you have not seen and which you should certainly have visited before bestowing your favours on the Laird of Cowan!"

So he knew already where she had been, Clova thought, and the manner in which he spoke told her how much it had infuriated him.

In a voice which she hoped was impersonal she said:

"I intend to visit all our neighbours one by one to make sure that the feuds between our Clans are settled, and I also intend, Cousin Euan, to tell our own people that any aggressive action against other Clansmen will be severely punished."

"And how will you punish them?" Euan enquired.

Clova did not answer, and he went on:

"I must inform you that the dungeons in this Castle have been used for some time as cellars or storerooms, and are no longer suitable for prisoners. But I have one at Mallic which I could lend you, and which would be a very effective deterrent to any intending criminal."

Clova knew he was mocking at her authority, and after a moment she said:

"What I have said is not a light threat, Cousin Euan. I intend to call a meeting of the Elders to help me consider what we should do with any offenders who ignore my instructions, and especially those who incite them to crimes that are not only provocative, but cruel and heartless."

Euan threw back his head and laughed.

"Very dramatic, my pretty Cousin, and of course, entirely commendable! The only thing is, as you well know, you have to catch your fish before you can eat it."

They had reached the top of the staircase and he walked away from her, his kilt swinging defiantly as he did so.

"I hate him!" Clova said again.

At the same time, she knew that he was not in the least intimidated by her and was doubtless already cogitating in his own mind some cruel and unpleasant plan for which it would be very difficult to find the person responsible.

She was so perturbed by Euan's obvious intentions that she sent a servant to the village to ask Torbot McBlane to come to see her.

He did not arrive until after tea, when Clova was beginning to think her message could not have reached him.

As soon as he appeared she took him quickly into the Library because the General and his wife were in the Chieftain's Room.

Although there was no sign of Euan, she was well aware he was still staying in the Castle and might appear at any moment.

"I am sorry I could not come before, My Lady," Torbot McBlane said, "but I did not get your message until I returned home less than half-an-hour ago."

"It is very kind of you to come," Clova said.

They sat down in two comfortable arm-chairs and she explained to him that she had visited Castle Cowan with her Cousin Jamie earlier that morning.

Then she told him that she intended to visit other Clans bordering on their estate as soon as she learned who they were and if the Chieftain was in residence.

She then told him what the Laird of Cowan had told her to the effect that a young man wearing the McBlane tartan had been seen attempting to steal two newborn lambs from a ewe which had just given birth.

She knew from the expression on Torbot McBlane's face that he was well aware who had been the instigator of such a theft.

"I want you and the other Elders to decide what punishment should be given to any McBlane Clansmen who commit such an offence again," she said, "and to make sure that they are aware that they will be watched, and that I shall ask everybody who learns of such disgraceful behaviour to tell me or you what they know."

There was silence before Torbot McBlane said slowly:

"I think many of them would be afraid to give the information to you."

"What you are saying," Clova said sharply, "is that my Cousin Euan has such a hold over the people that they dare not offend him."

Torbot McBlane nodded.

"That is true, for whenever in the past he has quarrelled with any Clansmen or they have offended him in some way, they have always suffered and their families have suffered with them."

"I cannot believe it!" Clova exclaimed. "Surely you and the other Elders can prevent that from happening?"

"If a man is shot at when he is alone on the moors, or a woman comes home to find the windows of her cottage are broken or its thatched roof has caught fire, it is difficult to point the finger at any one person."

"But it has to be stopped, it must be!" Clova said.

"We have tried in the past," Torbot McBlane replied, "and with your help, My Lady, we will try harder, but you must take care of yourself."

"Are you suggesting my life is in danger?"

She knew he thought before he spoke, then he said:

"It might be. A farmer who caught one of the gang and beat him for harassing his sheep also arranged to take him before the Magistrates, but before the case could be heard he was found drowned in the Loch near where he lived. He was far out on the water when his boat sprang a leak and he could not swim."

Clova drew in her breath.

"There are ways," Torbot McBlane went on, "of drilling a hole in a fishing-boat and filling it with sugar, which slowly dissolves when it becomes wet. Then when it has done so, the boat fills with water and sinks."

"That is wicked—diabolical!" Clova exclaimed.

"Now, you must not upset yourself, My Lady," Torbot said. "We, the Elders, will fight on your behalf to put an end to this mischief once and for all!"

"It is something we cannot allow."

"I agree," Torbot McBlane replied.

But she knew that he felt as helpless as she did.

Euan was clever, very clever, and the land was so sparsely populated that a crime could take place without anyone hearing the cries of a victim or seeing what occurred.

As she went up to dress for dinner, Clova found Jeanne was aware that she had visited Castle Cowan.

"Oi could hardly believe ye would do anything so unusual, M'Lady," she said. "Ever since Oi were born, Oi've been told to have naught t' do with th' McCowans. It's been hard at times, seeing that many of them are fine upstanding young laddies, and there be a shortage here on th' Strath of younger men."

"Why is that?" Clova enquired.

"Some o' them joined Highland Regiments, others find it difficult to get work, so they move t' Edinburgh or Glasgow, then send money hame t' their parents."

"So the girls want to know the McCowans?" Clova said. "Well, I hope that will be possible in the future."

"Not if Mr. Euan has anything to do with it," Jeanne replied, then put her hand over her mouth.

"I should not have said that, M'Lady," she said in a frightened voice. "Please forget it."

She glanced over her shoulder as she spoke as if, even when they were in the privacy of Clova's own bedroom, there might be somebody to overhear and repeat what she had said to Euan McBlane, who seemed to have assumed such authority over them.

"This has got to stop!" Clova told herself.

At the same time, as she went into dinner she felt apprehensive and uncertain of herself.

Euan, resplendent in his evening-clothes, with a lace jabot at his throat and wearing the magnificent sporran of a Chieftain to which he was not entitled, set himself out to be charming.

There were only four of them in the large Dining-Room, waited on by three kilted servants, and Euan made them laugh with his stories of the McBlane family.

As both the food and wine were excellent, Clova knew the General and his wife were enjoying themselves.

Then at the end of dinner the Piper came in to play the tunes that they all knew as he walked round and round the table, and when he eventually stopped at Clova's side, she offered him a small gold cup which had been set down in front of her filled with whisky.

He toasted her in Gaelic and she said "thank you" in the same language.

Then as he walked out, she saw the expression on Euan's face, and knew it was one of hatred and envy because she was the Chieftain and not he.

"He hates me as much as I hate him!" she told herself, and felt a shiver run through her body, as if a ghost had walked over her grave.

chapter six

AFTER dinner the General and his wife talked for a little while to Clova while Euan disappeared, and she wondered vaguely what he was doing.

He came back just as Lady McBlane had risen to her feet and said:

"I think I must take Robert to bed. It has been quite a tiring day talking to so many of our relatives, and I know he wants to start off early tomorrow morning and try to catch a salmon."

"That is a good idea!" Clova said. "I hope, Cousin Robert, you will let me come with you."

"Of course," the General replied, "but even if you knew how to fish as a child, you may have forgotten it after all these years."

"I remember fishing with a trout rod when I was small, and I am sure if you show me what to do I will soon pick it up again."

Lady McBlane collected her embroidery and said:

"One person who will not come with you, Robert, is me, because if there is anything I find really boring, it is to watch other people fishing!"

The General laughed.

"That is not the right attitude for a Scottish lass, and you must not set Clova a bad example."

"I think Clova is going to be a good example to us all," Lady McBlane replied.

She kissed her as she spoke and said:

"Goodnight, my child. We are very proud of you, and no one could have done better than you did yesterday."

Clova smiled, then knowing it would be a mistake to be alone with Euan, she followed them out through the door.

As she passed he said:

"I suppose, Cousin Clova, you would not like to come and look at the moonlight with me? It is one of the sights we always show our visitors."

"I will think about that tomorrow night," Clova answered. "At the moment I am feeling rather stiff after my ride."

She thought he intended to say something rude or sarcastic about her riding over to Castle Cowan, and she therefore hurried quickly after the General and his wife, keeping close to them until she reached her bedroom.

Jeanne was not there, presumably because Clova had come up earlier than she had expected.

Instead of ringing the bell for her, Clova went to the window to pull back the curtains and look out.

As Euan had said, the moonlight over the Strath was very beautiful.

In the daytime there were lights on the moors which were different from anything Clova had ever seen before.

Now the Strath was silver under a sky filled with stars, and it was a breath-taking sight.

The beauty of it filled her with an irrepressible rapture, and she stood looking out for a long time, wishing she could share what she was feeling with somebody else.

She could not pretend even to herself that it was not Tarquil Cowan with whom she wanted to share it.

She wondered if he, too, was looking out of his window, thinking of her, and she felt her thoughts fly towards him on wings and she was sure he understood.

At the same time, despairingly she had the feeling he would never declare to her his inner feelings.

He would have too much pride to expose himself to the imputation of being a fortune-hunter.

It was then that she faced the truth: that although it seemed incredible, she loved a man she had seen only twice in her life.

This was love as she had always wanted to find it, but now there were obstacles in the way that were far more difficult than anything her mother had encountered.

She half-suspected, although she did not like to express it to herself, that the feeling Lottie had had for the many men who had come and gone in her life had been very light and superficial, even if she had been upset when they left her.

In fact, after Lionel Arkwright had gone back to England, she had wept bitter tears.

But to Lottie life was like champagne, and as long as she could laugh and there were people to admire and pay her compliments, she found a happiness which was very different from what Clova wanted.

She knew it was not only love that she required from a man, but that he should be somebody to whom she could talk, on who she could rely, and who would protect and guide her.

She was sure, too, that the vibrations she had felt mingling with hers from the moment she had first met Tarquil were an expression of true love that came from her heart and his.

When he had talked to her and when he had pledged himself to her service, the expression in his eyes has not been one of a man who just desired a pretty woman.

It was something far deeper, far more sincere, far more fundamental.

"I love him!" she whispered to the moonlight, and prayed he was saying the same thing about her.

The door opened behind her and Jeanne came into the room.

"Why did ye not ring for me, M'Lady? I would'na have known ye had come to your bed if I'd not seen that the lights in the Chieftain's Room had been blown out."

"I am tired, Jeanne," Clova replied, "but I was thinking how beautiful the moonlight is."

"Beautiful to us, M'Lady," Jeanne said, "but strange things happen when the moon be high which makes some people afeared!"

Clova did not reply.

She knew Jeanne was telling her that moonlight enabled the members of Euan's gang to find the sheep when they were resting, or giving birth, and track down cattle which could not be seen in the dark.

She tried to listen, but her thoughts were elsewhere as Jeanne came towards her to undo her gown.

She had just unfastened the first button when there was a knock on the door.

Clova turned her head in surprise as Jeanne went to answer it.

She had a conversation with a man in the passage which Clova could not hear.

Then she came back to say:

"Somebody has called an' is asking to see ye, M'Lady. Shall I say you're too tired?"

"Who is it?" Clova enquired.

"It's a man who has brought his mother with him in a carriage. He says she's awful ill and she must speak with ye."

Clova hesitated, then remembered she was the Chieftain and she had told the Clansmen to come to her whenever they needed help.

"I must go down, Jeanne."

Jeanne picked up a pretty evening shawl that Clova had bought in Paris, thinking she would need it in the winter, and put it around her shoulders.

"If ye're going to the door, M'Lady," she said, "the wind is awful chilly at this time o' the night."

"I hope I shall not be long," Clova replied.

She walked out into the passage and found that instead of a senior servant, who was called Dougall, there was only a young man, one of the footmen, who Clova had thought was rather slow-witted, waiting for her.

"Who has called to see me, Andrew?" she asked.

"Ah dinna k-ken, Ma'am," he stammered.

Clova walked quickly along the passage and down the stairs into the hall.

The lights had been extinguished except for just one lantern which made the hall seem filled with shadows.

The door, however, was ajar, and she could see a young man with untidy hair and wearing a ragged kilt standing outside, a carriage behind him.

"You wanted to see me?" Clova enquired.

He made a somewhat awkward bow and said:

"'Tis ma mither, Ma'am. She be awfu' bad, but she would ha' a word wi' ye afore she dies."

"If she is as ill as that," Clova said, "she should not be travelling at this time of night."

She walked down the steps and the man followed her to open the carriage-door as she reached it.

Then as she peered into the darkness she felt him give her a tremendous push from behind as she sprawled forward into the carriage.

The door was shut and instantly the horses started off.

For a moment Clova could not believe what was actually happening.

Then as she tried to raise herself from the floor a plaid came over her head enveloping her in darkness.

A man's arms dragged her onto the seat of the carriage.

As she tried to struggle, a rope was fastened around her body holding her arms pinioned to her sides so that she was unable to raise the plaid from her face.

Then she was pushed into a corner of the back

seat, and to her horror she suspected who the man sitting next to her was.

As her heart beat frantically she realised she had been kidnapped from her own Castle and there was no point in asking who had done it.

Euan was abducting her, and even if it were not he who was sitting next to her, she was sure this was his plot, carried out on his instructions.

The horses were being driven at a wild speed, which made the carriage swing from side to side and bump uncomfortably over any unevenness in the road.

Clova realised they were going North and she knew that Mallic, Euan's Castle, was about three miles from Strathblane.

She had heard the General say conversationally at Luncheon that the relation who had the shortest distance to travel was Euan.

Because the plaid that covered her face was of thick wool, Clova knew it was no use her screaming or trying to speak.

She was being thrown about in the back of the carriage, since with her arms pinioned she could not steady herself, and found herself every so often bumping against the shoulder of the man who sat next to her.

It was horrifying and humiliating that she should be treated in such a manner, and she was also desperately afraid of what Euan was planning.

If he was hiding her away, she knew there was nothing she would be able to do about it, and no one to save her.

Because she was growing more and more frightened, she found herself praying not only to God for help, but also to Tarquil.

"Save me! Save...me!" she cried. "You... anticipated that he... might do this. How can I make you... realise how much I... want you?"

She knew then she loved Tarquil even more than she thought she did when she was looking out of the window at the moonlight.

She loved him because he was strong and yet gentle, and he cared for those who were dependent upon him.

He was in every way the sort of man she had always wanted to meet.

Because of the strange life she had lived with her mother, Clova had become a very good judge of men, and she had known as soon as each one approached Lottie exactly what he was like.

She knew what they would say, how they would treat her mother, and she was always proved right, with everything happening exactly as she expected.

She was sure now that Tarquil was good in every way. He was not just a man who was looking out for a bit of fun like those who whether they were French, English, South African, or any other nationality, would only care for her mother so long as she amused them.

When the novelty and the excitement was over, they would disappear and presumably forget her.

When she was in Paris, Clova had sworn that would never happen to her!

She would never marry anybody unless he loved her in a very different way, so that his love would grow rather than fade in the years they were together.

Often she thought she was asking the impossible

and that all men were superficial and did not really care, as long as they found amusement, whom they hurt or who suffered when they were no longer interested.

But Tarquil was different.

He had asked her to trust him, and she knew she did trust him, and only he could save her now.

They must have driven a little over half-an-hour though it seemed very much longer, and Clova was feeling suffocated by the thickness of the plaid when the horses came to a standstill.

Now her heart was beating more frantically than ever, and she knew the fear inside her had been growing until all she wanted to do was to scream and go on screaming until somebody came to her rescue.

She heard the door of the carriage being opened, and then the man who had been sitting beside her lifted her up and passed her out to another man outside.

She was carried over some rough gravel which crunched beneath his feet up some steps.

Then she heard a voice that was undoubtedly Euan's saying in an authoritative tone:

"Carry her up to the tower!"

Now she was being taken up some stone stairs, along a corridor, then there were more stairs, small ones, and she was sure it was a narrow staircase because her captor carried her more upright in case her head or her knees should bang against the walls on either side.

There were, however, far fewer stairs than she had expected before she was set down and the rope which had pinioned her arms to her sides was undone.

It had been tied so tight that until her circulation was restored it was difficult to move her hands.

Then the plaid was raised from her face and for a second she could see nothing except that she was aware that the room, if that was what she was in, was lighter than the darkness she had endured under the thickness of the plaid.

She heard a door being closed, and as she put up her hand to sweep back her hair from her forehead she saw Cousin Euan standing watching her with his back to an empty fireplace.

Now she realised she was in a small round room with an oak bedstead on which she was sitting and no other furniture except for a wooden chair, and a table against one wall which held a basin and a ewer.

With a superhuman effort Clova found her voice.

"How dare you . . . bring me . . . here in this . . . disgraceful fashion!"

She meant to sound angry and peremptory, but in fact, being very frightened, she found it difficult to breathe properly; she merely sounded weak and very helpless.

"I brought you here," Euan replied, "because I have no intention of being kept waiting while you play about with our traditional enemies and think you can be a more effective Chieftain than I would be."

Clova wanted to stand up and defy him, but she was so stiff and her legs felt so weak that she found it impossible.

But she managed to lift her chin proudly and ask in what she hoped was a scornful voice:

"So you . . . intend to . . . kill me!"

"I did think of it," Euan admitted, "but because I

need your money and am sure if some interfering old fool of a Bank Manager, or perhaps Torbot McBlane, persuaded you in Paris to make a Will, I had a better idea."

"I suppose I must be... curious enough to... ask you... what it is," Clova said.

"I have every intention of telling you," Euan replied. "As I have already said, I intend to marry you, but you are obviously going to make difficulties, and although I could overcome them quite easily, I am in a hurry."

"Why?"

"The answer is easy, my dear Cousin," Euan answered. "I am in debt, and although I have informed my creditors that I will soon have a very rich wife, they prefer proof rather than promises."

"In which case they will be... disappointed!" Clova said. "For I have... no intention of... marrying you."

"I gave you the opportunity of accepting me," Euan said, "but you did not take it, and now you have no choice."

"Do you really think that you can... kidnap me in this... disgraceful way," Clova asked, "and no one will... enquire what has... happened to me?"

"Of course they will," Euan agreed, "and I know that if I keep you here all night in my dungeons, which are infested with rats, you will certainly feel different in the morning."

Despite her resolution not to let him think she was afraid, Clova felt herself shiver.

She had always been terrified of rats, and once when she and Lottie had been in such poor lodgings that there were rats in the walls, she lay awake all night in terror in case she should feel them running over her bed.

As if Euan sensed what she was thinking, he gave a short laugh and said:

"At least I am sparing you that torture and also the other idea I had."

Clova did not speak, and after a moment he said:

"Are you not eager to know what that was? I will tell you. I thought if I raped you, you would have a child, and there would be no question then of your not marrying the father."

Clova gave a cry of horror that seemed to echo around the walls.

"How can you...think of...anything so... degrading...so disgusting...so wicked?" she cried. "One day, you will...suffer for the...crimes you have...committed!"

Euan laughed and it was an unpleasant sound.

"First they will have to catch me," he said, "and that is something, my smart little Cousin from Paris, you will be unable to do! And even if you do discover a great deal more about me than you know already, you must remember that a wife cannot give evidence against her husband in a Court of Law."

"I will not...marry you! I would rather...die than do...so!" Clova flashed.

"On the contrary, you will marry me, and you will help me spend your money in a far more enjoyable way than wasting it on a lot of ragged, illiterate Scots who should have been sent off to Canada with their forebears."

Clova gasped at the horror of what he was saying.

"How can you speak like that?" she asked. "You

are a McBlane, and every McBlane has always been proud of his Clan and of his country."

"What is there to be proud of?" Euan asked. "Acres of heather which bring in little money, sheep which sell for half the price of those from England, and cattle so undersized that they fetch a pittance in the market!"

His voice seemed to vibrate around the room as he went on.

"What I want is the pleasures and delights of London and the joys of Paris, which I am sure I need not explain to you. I also want to be able to travel like a gentleman in comfort and luxury anywhere in the world that pleases me."

There was an elated note in his voice now, and as he continued he bent down towards her which made her tremble.

"Only you, pretty Clova," he said, "can provide for me the life I want, and therefore, of course, you are very valuable to me. So I will not kill you, nor will I torture you unbearably."

"What do you . . . intend to . . . do?" Clova asked, and her voice was hardly above a whisper.

"I intend to do nothing more unpleasant than keep you here for the night with me," Euan replied. "There will be no escape, and when you are found missing in the morning everybody at Strathblane will learn where you have been."

He saw that Clova did not understand, and he went on mockingly.

"No one will really be surprised. They will just think you are following in the footsteps of your mother, who was nothing more than a harlot, and ran after any man who would pay her."

"How dare you say such . . . wicked and . . . untrue things!" Clova tried to say, but Euan continued as if she had not spoken.

"They will believe—and I shall make quite certain that they do believe—that you could not wait until we were married to enjoy my kisses and the uniting of our bodies. Therefore, my charming Cousin, you will be only too grateful when I offer you marriage, for it is unlikely any other man would be willing to do so in the circumstances."

It was now that Clova rose to her feet and walked towards him.

"Can you really . . . credit that I would marry you in such . . . circumstances, or that anyone would . . . believe . . . anything like that about . . . me?"

"Of course they will believe it," Euan said. "Wake up and be your age, Clova! You are tainted with your mother's sins, and you should face the fact that no decent man would want to marry the daughter of a woman with your mother's reputation."

He gave an evil chuckle as he said:

"Can you see the faces of that holy and pious Torbot and the rest of them when they learn tomorrow that their young and supposedly innocent Chieftain has been rolling about all night with me in the matrimonial bed without a gold band on her finger?"

"As they are already aware of your appalling deeds of violence," Clova flashed, "when I tell them the truth they will believe me."

"Then you do not know your Clansmen as well as I do," Euan mocked. "You may claim you were kept here as a prisoner, but if I am as bad as they think I am, is it likely that they will believe you have emerged from a night alone with a man like me unscathed and still the pure little pet whom they accepted as the Chieftain, even though she came from Paris?"

His eyes were on Clova's face as he said:

"The Scots never forget: your mother is still spoken of in whispers and doubtless her soul is prayed for in the *Kirk*."

He laughed evilly and went on.

"You will be put in the same category: a scarlet woman in the eyes of those who are prepared to turn their own children out into the snow if they have broken any of the Commandments, and who are more sanctimonious and pious than any other people on earth."

Euan threw out his hands as he finished speaking and said:

"God preserve me from the lot of them! We will leave Scotland, you and I, Clova, and enjoy ourselves among the flesh-pots, and when we do return, I will take your place as Chieftain."

He paused before he said reflectively:

"The Castle will be an amusing place in which to entertain shooting-parties in the Autumn. Then for the rest of the year, with your money to spend, the world is our oyster."

His voice seemed to echo around the small room, and Clova clutched her fingers together until the knuckles showed white.

Then she said slowly and stubbornly:

"Whatever... happens, I will not... marry you!"

"You would prefer that I take you down now, and shut you up in my dungeons?" Euan asked. "I think, when the rats have nibbled your toes and perhaps climbed up your skirts and onto your bare neck, you will scream for me to release you."

Despite her resolution not to do so, Clova shivered and knew she was terrified.

"You will stay here as I have arranged," he said sharply. "There is no escape from this room until I release you in the morning. Then, to save your face and of course mine, you will swear in front of my Factor, who will call on me at breakfast time, and my senior servant, that we are man and wife."

He chuckled.

"That is *'Marriage by Consent,'* and although it will undoubtedly shock the Elders that you did not wait to enjoy the lusts of the flesh until we were married in a *Kirk*, we will have a ceremony performed by a Minister within a few days."

"No . . . no. . . . " Clova murmured.

"The Clan can enjoy another roasted ox and drink themselves unconscious on whisky which you can well afford. After that, we will leave for our honeymoon in the South."

"If you . . . touch me . . . I will . . . kill myself!" Clova cried.

She glanced towards the window as she spoke, and her voice was hysterical.

Euan regarded her through half-closed eyes and almost as if he were speaking she knew he was considering whether he should rape her or not.

He might be thinking that if in the morning she was distraught and dishevelled, she might evoke pity rather than condemnation.

He was working it out as if it were a mathematical puzzle, and as she turned to face him defiantly he said:

"One day you will beg me for my favours, and

even if you dislike me, it will only make it more amusing for me to subdue you. Complacency can be a bore."

"You appall and disgust me!" Clova screamed.

For a moment she thought he would fling himself on her, and she wondered wildly how long she could fight him.

Then to her utter relief he walked towards the door.

"It may reassure you to know," he said, "that for tonight, at any rate, I will not touch you. Later I will certainly fulfil my duties as a husband to my satisfaction—and yours—but tonight you can sleep peacefully and alone."

He opened the door and said:

"Goodnight, Cousin Clova! When you think it over, you will find that it is easiest for you, and in your best interests, to accept my decision in this as in everything else. I intend to make sure that you make me a pleasant and obedient wife, so that there will be no need for any more dramatics."

His voice was threatening as he added:

"If there are, I assure you you will suffer for them, and it will amuse me to beat you to submission."

He left the room as he finished speaking, and as he shut the door Clova heard him turn the key in the lock and also press home a bolt.

Then there was just his footsteps going down the stone staircase and she was alone.

Because she knew she was utterly defeated she sank down on the floor and put her head down in her hands.

She could hardly believe this had happened to her.

Yet, while every nerve in her body revolted against what Euan had planned, she could see that in the twisted way in which his brain worked that it was very clever.

He was quite sure that nothing she could say in her defence would be accepted, and the fact that she had stayed the night alone in Mallic Castle with Euan would damn her in the eyes of the Clan forever.

She would have been very stupid if she had not been aware when she was coming back to Scotland that she had to live down her mother's reputation.

It was not only that Lottie had run away with a man who was a guest of her father-in-law, the Chieftain, but stories of her success in Paris would certainly have percolated back to Strathblane, doubtless many of them carried by Euan himself.

Clova had learnt from her other relatives that he had spent a great deal of time in France, and was not a sportsman as her father had been.

Nor, as she knew now, had he any fondness or loyalty for Scotland.

"He is ... utterly and ... completely ... despicable!" she whispered.

At the same time, if she did not marry him, she had the frightening feeling that the Clan might repudiate her.

Although it was very unusual, she was sure it was not impossible for them to refuse to serve under somebody they thought unworthy of their allegiance, especially if it was a woman, and there were a number of other Cousins, like Jamie, whom they could invite to become their Chieftain.

"What ... can I ... do? Oh, God ... what can I ... do?" she wondered.

She could only be thankful that Euan had left her alone, although it was not out of consideration for her, but merely in order that in the morning her promiscuous behaviour would be obvious to the Clan.

Tomorrow might be different.

Tomorrow, when she would be forced to acknowledge him as her husband, he would violate her, just as he would do everything possible to get her money into his own hands.

Although under the Law everything she possessed would become his, there would doubtless be documents to sign, and because Jan Maskill's Will was being proved in Paris, her agreement might be important.

The idea of what would happen once she was married was so terrifying that she rose from her knees to walk about the room, feeling, light though she was, the old floorboards creak under her feet.

She was aware that everything in the tower was dusty and dirty and had probably had not been cleaned for years.

She saw now that the bed was not made up and there was just a shabby mattress on the heavy oak frame, and two thin, almost threadbare blankets.

It was quite irrelevant, but she knew the bed had been made from the fir-trees that grew in the Strath.

She thought perhaps the whole Castle had been furnished on the estate by Euan's ancestors, who once cared for the McBlane Clansmen, and employed them where it was possible.

What he wanted, as he had said, was the exciting pleasures he could find in London and Paris.

Knowing how wicked he was, Clova was sure he indulged in the vices she had tried not to think about when she was with her mother.

"How could I...live with...such a man?" she asked aloud.

Because the very idea was so horrifying, she went to the window to throw open one of the small casements and see if by some miracle she could escape that way.

She saw then that the Castle stood on the very edge of a cliff.

During the centuries since it had been built, the sea had eroded much of the rock below it, so that now from the window out of which she was looking there was almost a straight drop down to the sea.

Below the cliffs were rugged rocks over which the waves were breaking.

The tower, she was sure, was the oldest part of the Castle, and the rest of it, which as she vaguely remembered somebody saying had been restored some fifty years ago, stretched inland from it.

There was certainly no escape for her there, and she looked up at the stars and wondered if she was brave enough to throw herself into the sea.

There was no question that if she did so, she would die instantly, and that seemed the only solution to her problems.

Because, however, in the moonlight the sea looked cold and dark, and the rocks even sharper and more dangerous than they did in the daytime, something young and resilient within her told her that life was very precious.

Yesterday when she had spoken to the Clan she had been so happy.

Yesterday she knew that at last she had a home, somewhere she belonged, and she was among people who accepted her as their own.

Now because she was rich, everything was to be taken from her.

She felt like cursing the diamond shares which Jan Maskill had left to her mother because she had given him a fleeting happiness, and which had multiplied until they had become an enormous fortune.

They would, *Monsieur* Beauvais had told her, doubtless increase in value even more in the future because the Mine was reported as showing a huge profit, year after year.

"If only Mama could have... enjoyed it," Clova whispered.

Then almost as if she were standing behind her she heard Lottie's happy, lilting laugh, and heard her say as she had so often when they were in trouble:

"Never say die! There is always tomorrow, and the dawn of a new day."

It had been Lottie's whole philosophy that there was always something better around the corner, and yet, when Clova thought of Euan waiting for her like an evil ogre, she could think of nothing more terrifying than that she should be his wife.

She was certain, too, that once he had got what he wanted, all her money into his hands, he would dispose of her very effectively in such a manner that the crime would never be attributed to him.

"What shall I do, Mama?" she asked like a child who was frightened of the dark, and she was almost certain she heard Lottie laugh again.

Because it was cold in the tower and because, too, her whole body ached not only from riding, but from being bumped about in the carriage that had brought her here, she lay down on the bed and pulled the inadequate blankets over her.

She knew she would not sleep, but at least she could rest so that she had all her faculties working in the morning, and could try, although it seemed impossible, to find a way of circumventing Euan's ghastly plan.

"Help me! Please, help me!" she whispered, and knew that once again it was a prayer flying out to Tarquil Cowan.

Even to think of him brought her a sense of comfort, and she could feel the strength of his arms as he had lifted her down from her horse and see the expression in his eyes when they talked together in his Castle.

"I love him! I love him! But he, too, will believe Euan and will never wish to speak to me again!" she cried.

* * *

It was a long time later when she heard a strange sound.

It flashed through her mind that it was a rat that had scampered across the floor, she stifled the scream that rose to her lips.

Every story she had ever heard of rats, which when they were hungry had eaten babies and bitten prisoners or small children, ran through her mind.

Then when the sound came again she sat up.

The moon was now at its full height and its light was streaming through the uncurtained windows to cast a glow of silver over the whole room.

When she got into bed, Clova had not blown out

the candle which had been alight when the plaid was taken off her head, but had left it burning on the chair beside her bed, as there was no table.

Now it was guttering low, and there was no need for it because the moonlight lit the room as if it were the light of day.

Then as she sat trembling, looking around for the sign of the rat running across the uncarpeted floor, she realised the sound had come from the window.

A moment later she saw two hands grasping the window-ledge of the casement she had left open.

Then there was the head of a man, and Clova thought she was dreaming, but as she stared, too astonished even to scream, he raised himself up farther, and put one leg inside the window.

Then she knew as his body followed it that it was Tarquil.

She gave a little cry of joy and irrepressible happiness as she sprang out of the bed and ran towards him.

Then as he pulled himself into the room she flung herself against him.

"You have ... come! You ... have come! How did you ... know? How did ... you hear ... me? I have been praying ... desperately, but I never thought you would ... know ... where I was!"

His arms went around her, and as she looked up at him, tears of relief ran down her cheeks, and with her hair falling over her shoulders she looked very beautiful.

For a moment he just looked at her, then his arms tightened and his mouth came down on hers and held her captive.

It was then Clova realised it was true, he was

135

there and would save her.

But even that joy was lost in the thrill of his kiss and the feeling of rapture that swept over her.

Now her love that she had acknowledged to herself seemed to rise within her and pour itself out towards him.

As he kissed her she moved closer to him until she felt they were joined invisibly and she was no longer herself, but part of him.

Only when he raised his head did she say incoherently:

"I love...you! I love...you!"

"And I love you, my darling," he said in a voice which was very deep and moving, "but before we do anything else, I have got to get you quickly out of this terrible place."

"The door is...locked and...bolted," Clova said, "and he will not let me go...I am sure he... will not let me go."

There was a note of stark terror in her voice which made Tarquil pull her roughly to him.

"I have to get you away," he said, "and to do so you have to be very brave. Moreover, we must not talk, as voices carry at night."

As if to make sure she did not do so, he kissed her once again.

Then when it was impossible to think of anything but the rapture he had aroused in her, he put her resolutely from him and started to unwind the rope which was around her body.

He looked around the room, saw the oak bedstead, and with an exclamation which told Clova he was pleased, he walked towards it and tied the rope firmly around one of the legs, which was very sturdy.

Then Clova realised that as he moved there was another rope hanging behind him outside the window.

It was then she knew what he intended to do and remembered how frightening the fall to the sea had looked.

Now she could see outside that standing back from the rocks and moving up and down on the waves there was a boat with a man in it.

When he had tied the rope to his satisfaction, Tarquil came back to her side.

"Are you brave enough, my darling," he asked, "to climb down the rope?"

Without answering him Clova looked out the window and gave a shudder.

The sea seemed an immense distance away and she answered in a whisper:

"Y-you will think me a...coward...but I... could not...d-do it."

He smiled.

"That is what I expected you to say, so we will risk it together."

He drew her closer to him, then taking the scarf from around his neck, which was much longer than a man usually wore, he put it around his own waist, then around hers, tying them together.

Then he said quietly but firmly:

"Now you have to trust me. Put your arms around my neck but take care not to throttle me, shut your eyes, and just pray that God will carry us to safety, and away from that devil who has brought you here."

"I am...praying," Clova said.

He kissed her forehead before he lifted her up in his arms.

chapter seven

CLOVA kept her eyes shut and prayed as Tarquil had told her to do.

She was aware that he was letting himself down the wall of the Castle in the same way as a mountaineer climbed or descended a cliff.

He found precarious foot-holds in the rough stones, and his hands, immensely strong, clenched the rope.

She was sensible enough to control her impulse to hold him tightly round his neck in case it might throttle him.

At the same time, she knew that if she opened her eyes, she would be so frightened that she might either scream or faint.

"Please... God... please... get us away safely please... please..."

She was praying with an intensity which made her

feel as if her whole body, her mind, and her soul went into her prayer.

Then she was aware that they had now got down to the top of the cliff, and Tarquil was finding it even more difficult to descend onto the rocks.

'Supposing we . . . fall into the . . . sea and are . . . drowned?'

Now Clova was praying again, praying until it was a distant shock when she felt a jar as Tarquil's feet touched the rocks.

He did not speak, he only undid the scarf that bound them together, and dropping down between two rocks, he pulled her into his arms.

He was standing in water up to his knees and as he moved slowly forward the waves splashed over them both, and at the same time brought the boat nearer to them.

As it rocked awkwardly Tarquil dropped her into the stern, swung himself into the boat, and sitting down, he seized a pair of oars and started to row as the man who had been waiting for them was doing.

Clova, holding on to the sides of the boat, raised herself to a sitting position, and as she did so she looked back at the Castle and gave a cry of fear.

Climbing down the rope which they had left behind them was Euan.

Somehow he must have heard them, or perhaps some instinct had told him of her escape.

Now he was following her and, although she was not certain what he could do since they were already moving out to sea, she was afraid.

"It is all right," Tarquil said comfortingly, "he will not be able to stop us now."

He was facing her in the boat and as she looked

up at him beseechingly, still so terrified by all she had gone through that it was difficult to think coherently, she saw the man behind him put down his oars and pick up a rifle from the bottom of the boat.

He raised it to his shoulder, and only as he pointed at Euan did Clova realise he was about to shoot him.

She felt she must order him not to do so, but the words would not come to her lips.

She only heard herself murmur feebly:

"No! No!"

Then the man fired and Clova saw that the bullet had struck well above Euan's head and he was already half-way down the side of the Castle.

'He has missed,' she thought, and did not know whether to be glad or sorry.

Tarquil, who had been looking at her face, did not realise what was happening until he heard the explosion behind him.

He turned his head just as the man behind him re-loaded with the swiftness of long practice and raised the rifle again.

"No, Angus!" he said sharply.

But it was too late.

There was a second explosion from the rifle which was almost drowned by the sound of the waves, and once again Clova realised he had fired several feet above Euan's head, exactly as he had done before.

Knowing now he was in great danger, Euan swung out on the rope.

Clova realised that the man in the boat, who she guessed from his use of the rifle to be a stalker, was firing not at Euan himself, but at the rope on which he was swinging.

At the same moment the impact of the two bullets

and the sudden pressure that Euan had exerted on it caused the rope to break.

It did so just as he reached the top of the cliff and aware that he had now lost the support of the rope, he struggled to find a footing on the rough edge but failed.

The broken rope swinging down added to his instability, and clutching wildly at the air he fell over the edge of the cliff, crashing down onto the rocks beneath.

As Clova gave a cry of horror seeing him lying there spread-eagled, his hands flung out in front of him, a huge wave breaking over the rock on which he had fallen swept him into the sea.

For a moment she could see his head emerging above the foam. Then the wave receded and there was no further sight of him.

Tarquil did not speak, neither did the stalker, but they started to row quickly and expertly away from the breaking waves.

They headed South under the shelter of the land until Clova saw ahead of them the mouth of the river which ran through the Strath.

Just before reaching it they were for a short time in the open sea without the protection of the cliffs, and she was aware a storm was rising and the wind coming from the North was very strong.

Every moment the sea was growing more and more turbulent, but they managed to reach safely the small harbour which contained several fishing-boats, but showed no other sign of human habitation.

Angus pulled the boat alongside an iron ladder which led from the water-level to the Quay above it.

He held the boat steady as Tarquil helped Clova

onto the ladder, then followed her himself.

When he reached the top he looked back but did not speak, just waving his hand in a gesture of salute to the Stalker who replied similarly.

Tarquil hurried Clova along the Quay until at the end of it they reached a shed in which she saw there was a horse stabled.

They entered it, and now in the darkness and out of sight of anybody who might have seen them in the moonlight, Tarquil put his arms around her.

"You are safe, my precious! He can never frighten you again."

She was trembling as she hid her face against his shoulder.

"Is Cousin Euan . . . dead?" she murmured.

"He would have been unconscious when he hit the rock," Tarquil said. "The sea will have carried him away, and nothing is likely to be heard of him again for weeks, perhaps months, until he is washed up on some distant shore."

Clova gave a deep sigh, and he said:

"It is all over and now I am going to take you home."

He did not wait for her reply but picked her up in his arms, put her on the horse's back, then mounted behind her.

They both had to bend their heads as they rode out of the shed.

Tarquil moved quickly and carefully, keeping out of sight of the scattered crofts which were all shrouded in darkness.

Then they rode beside the river towards Strathblane Castle.

Because she could hardly believe that what had

occurred was true, Clova shut her eyes and with her cheek against the soft tweed of Tarquil's coat felt that it all must have been a nightmare.

Now she was safe, she was in his arms, and she could feel his heart beating against her breasts.

He rode in silence, intent, she knew, on getting her back as quickly as possible to the Castle.

She wished instead she were going with him to his own home and need not leave him.

"How could any man be so wonderful?" she asked herself.

She knew that no other man could have saved her in such a hazardous and daring manner.

Cousin Euan was dead, and although she thought it was wrong to be glad that anybody had died, yet, because he was no longer there to menace her or anybody else, it seemed sensible to know that the world would be a cleaner place because he was not in it.

But for the moment she could think of nothing except Tarquil.

All too quickly she realised that he had drawn his horse to a standstill, having brought her through the protecting fir-trees until she was within a very short distance of the Castle.

She opened her eyes and looked up at him.

Although the moonlight had waned a little, he could see the expression of love in her eyes and the trembling of her lips.

She felt his arms tighten as he said:

"You are safe, my darling, that is all that matters."

"I prayed to ... you," Clova said, "but I did not think it ... possible that ... anybody could ... save me."

"He did not hurt you or touch you?"

There was a sharp note in his voice which told her how much it mattered, and she quickly said:

"He ... he was intending to keep me there ... until tomorrow ... so that everybody would believe that I had ... gone with him willingly ... and we were immediately to be married by Consent ... so that there could then be ... no chance of my ... escaping."

"I thought he might do something like that!" Tarquil said angrily.

"H-how did you know? How ... were you ... aware?"

"My men were watching from the moors and from here in the trees," Tarquil answered. "I myself was only a short distance from the Castle when you were driven away by Euan's gang of young criminals."

"They told me," Clova murmured, "that there was an ... old woman who ... wanted to see me ... before she ... died."

"They knew you would not refuse that," Tarquil said, and for a moment his lips rested on her forehead.

"Suppose you had not ... come when you ... did? He would have ... forced me to ... marry him."

"If that had happened, I would have killed him with my bare hands!" Tarquil said. "But Angus has made sure that if his body is ever found, there will be no marks on it except for those he sustained from the rocks on which he fell."

"Then ... I really am ... free!"

"God heard your prayer," Tarquil answered. "Now, my little love, you must go back to the Castle and, if anybody sees you, make up some excuse for being out late. You know nothing—nothing of what has happened tonight, and the fact that your Cousin has disappeared will not, I think, perturb anyone."

His voice sharpened as he added:

"If people are curious, they will doubtless think he has gone off to find more exotic entertainment than is available in the Highlands."

As Tarquil finished speaking he swung himself down from the saddle, then lifted Clova to the ground beside him

Because she could not help herself, she clung to him, longing to tell him that she wanted to stay with him but knowing she had to obey his instructions.

He put his arm around her, then in a voice that was deep and hoarse he said:

"You are so beautiful, so absurdly, ridiculously beautiful that I find it difficult to believe you are real."

She felt her heart turn over at the depth of emotion behind his words and lifted her lips up to his.

He kissed her passionately, but at the same time she thought there was a kind of reverence in his kiss, as if he found her very precious.

Then as everything was forgotten in a sensation of ecstasy that was part of the moonlight, the stars, and the scent of the fir-trees, Tarquil released her. He turned her round gently so that she faced the Castle and said unsteadily:

"Go while I can let you, and God go with you!"

He gave her shoulders a little push as he spoke and she moved away from him, longing to turn round and run back, knowing he would expect her to obey him.

It took her only a few minutes to reach the front door.

She did not have to knock, as she guessed that Andrew, the young foreman, who was rather stupid, would when she did not return just go back to bed and leave the door open for her.

She hurried up the stairs. When she reached the top of them she took off her evening-slippers so that she made no sound as she walked down the carpeted corridor past the General and her Cousin Mary's bedroom.

She knew if she rang for Jeanne she might think it strange for her to have been gone for so long.

However, when she opened her bedroom door she saw in the light of the candles that were still burning on her dressing-table and by her bed, that Jeanne was lying back in an arm-chair beside the fireplace, fast asleep.

On tip-toe Clova walked across the room, blew out all the candles except one, then undressing quickly she got into bed.

Only when her head was on the pillow in the darkness was she aware of how desperately tired she was.

She did not want to think of what had occurred, or her fear and horror at what Euan had said to her!

She wanted to feel that Tarquil's arms were still around her and she was safe; safe because he had saved her and because he loved her.

"I love you! I love you!" she whispered into the darkness.

Then waves of exhaustion seemed to sweep over her and she knew no more . . .

* * *

Clova awoke and realised that the sun was shining into her bedroom through the sides of the curtains and she was alone.

Jeanne must have crept out without disturbing her, and she saw that her clothes were no longer where she had thrown them down when she undressed, but had been taken away.

She did not ring the bell but lay for a long time, thinking back over what had happened last night, and finding it so extraordinary that it was hard to believe it had all actually occurred.

She could still feel the horror of that dreadful drive with her face covered with the plaid, and the disgust and revulsion she had felt when Euan told her what he intended.

She could also remember her utter despair when she had felt there could be no escape.

Then Tarquil had come to her like a Knight of old saving a Princess from the Ogre's Castle or from the dragon.

He had carried her away, not on a white charger, but in his arms!

It was impossible not to feel a shiver go through her as she remembered the agony of their descent down from the Castle wall, then down the cliffs to where the boat was waiting for them.

"How could any man be so brave and at the same time so clever?" she asked herself.

Then as if by a miracle Euan had died when Angus the stalker had severed the rope which he, too, was using to pursue them by what Clova knew were two brilliant shots.

Euan was dead, her Clan was free of him and of his nefarious activities, and so was she.

"I am free! I am free!" she wanted to cry. "Free to love Tarquil, free to help my people and Scotland as I wish to do."

Because she could no longer lie thinking about it but felt she must start at once, she rang the bell for Jeanne, who came hurrying into her bedroom.

"How could Oi have done anythin' so awfu', M'Lady, as tae fall asleep while Oi was awaitin' for ye?" she asked. "Why did ye no wake me?"

"You were tired, and so was I," Clova smiled, "so I slipped into bed, and I never heard you leave the room."

"'Twas kind of ye and it's now nearly eleven o'clock, M'Lady. Oi let ye sleep after goin' so late to bed. Lady Mary has a headache and'll not wish to be disturbed, an' Sir Robert's gone fishing."

"Then there is no need for me to hurry," Clova said, "and I would like a bath."

It was nearly luncheon-time when she left her bedroom, and she wondered if Tarquil would come to see her before or after luncheon.

But there was no sign of him when it was announced that the meal was ready and she ate alone, waited on by Dougall and a young footman.

She felt rather small and insignificant in the huge Baronial Dining-Room with the life-sized portrait of her grandfather staring at her from the other side of the room.

'What I need is a . . . husband,' she thought, and felt herslf blush at the idea.

The sun was shining and after luncheon she would have liked to go for a walk in the garden and feel the warmth of it on her skin.

The wind that had blown furiously at dawn had

now subsided to a soft breeze, but she dared not leave the Castle in case Tarquil came and she missed him.

When at last he was announced, she was looking out of the window in the Chieftain's Room and she could not suppress a little cry of delight as he walked towards her.

She thought she had never seen him look more handsome or more distinguished.

She realized she was seeing him for the first time dressed as a Chieftain and not in the ordinary tweed jacket he had worn on other occasions.

Now there was something quite formal about him, and she thought, too, that his voice was somehow different as he asked:

"You are rested?"

"I slept late... and now I have been... waiting for... you."

"I have called, as you have asked me to do."

She felt there was something strange in the way he spoke, she looked at him a little puzzled as he stood at her side, the sunshine from the window illuminating his face and turning her hair into a halo of gold.

She waited, a question in her eyes, and after a moment Tarquil said, still in that strange voice she did not recognise:

"I want to talk to you, Clova."

She longed to reply that the one thing she wanted him to do was to kiss her.

Instead, she sat down on one of the red velvet window-seats and made a little gesture with her hand for him to join her.

He did so, turning sideways as she had done, so that in the carved seat they faced each other.

"Was everything all right when you returned?" he enquired.

"No one knew when I got back," Clova said quickly, feeling this was somehow unimportant. "The front door was open and Jeanne my maid was asleep in a chair in my bedroom and I did not wake her."

Tarquil nodded as if to show his satisfaction.

Then to Clova's surprise he looked away from her out through the window at the well-kept garden with its colourful flowers and beyond it to where the green fields stretched out along the Strath and down to the river.

She felt he was comparing it with his own land and asked quickly:

"Tarquil, what is ... wrong?"

"There is nothing wrong," he replied, "now that you are safe, and you can no longer be menaced by your cousin."

She did not speak and after a moment he went on.

"He has been the disturbing influence that has resulted in the continuing bitterness and feuding between our Clans. Now we can live in peace, and I am sure under your guidance the McBlanes will prosper."

Clova looked at him, puzzled by the way he was speaking and the fact that he was not looking at her.

She felt as if he had withdrawn a long distance from her.

While her whole being was vibrating towards him, yearning for him, he seemed to be unaware of it.

"You know without my saying it," Tarquil continued, "that I am at your service to help you in any way I can, but I think you will find that the McBlanes who live on the estate, and perhaps also those who have moved away, will be ready and willing to assist you, should you invite them to do so."

Clova felt as if an icy hand were clutching at her heart, and because she was frightened she asked impulsively as a child might have done:

"Why are you . . . talking to me . . . like this? What had I . . . done? Why do you . . . no longer . . . love me?"

The words seemed to burst from her lips, and as Tarquil turned to look at her he saw there was a stricken expression in her eyes and she was trembling.

He put out his hands towards her, but at once, as if deliberately controlling himself, he rose and walked away from the window.

Clova watched him, feeling as if when she had least expected it the ceiling had crashed down on her head, and the whole Castle lay in ruins at her feet.

Tarquil was standing in front of the huge fireplace, where the whole trunk of a tree could be burnt.

He looked up to where over it there was a portrait of Clova's great-grandfather, looking very impressive in a bonnet decorated with black cock's feathers on the side of his head.

He stared at it, then he said:

"You must understand my position. Surely there is no need for me to put it into words?"

"I do not . . . know what you are . . . saying to me," Clova said. "Last night . . ."

"Last night was exceptional, and something we both have to forget," Tarquil interposed.

"Why? Why should I forget that you saved me when I was in utter despair... and that you... told me that you... loved me?"

Her voice dropped as she said the last words, and yet he heard them.

"It is difficult to be sane and sensible in the circumstances in which we found ourselves."

There was silence, then Clova asked in a broken little voice:

"Are you... saying that you... you have changed your mind... and you... no longer... love me?"

It was the cry of a frightened child who found herself alone in the dark, and Tarquil clenched his fists before he replied:

"Of course not! I love you as I have never loved anyone in the whole of my life! But I have some pride left and some sense of decency, and you must be aware that I have nothing to offer you."

Clova gave a little cry.

"Are you... thinking of my... money?" she asked.

Now her voice had changed and she jumped up from where she was sitting and ran towards him.

She stood in front of him so that he was forced to look at her as she said:

"Do you... love me? Do you really... love me as you said you... did last... night?"

"I love you," Tarquil replied harshly, "but for God's sake do not make it harder for me than it is already."

"But I love you... Tarquil! I love... you with my... whole heart!"

He drew in his breath and she saw the pain in his eyes as he said:

"Will you try to understand that I am impoverished to the point where it is only by going without every luxury, at times even without proper food, that I can pay those who work for me."

There was a note of despair in his voice as he went on.

"However hard I try, I seem to sink deeper and deeper into debt, and if it were not for the fact that my people depend on me for their very existence, I would go to Edinburgh or Glasgow and find some lucrative work to do."

Clova did not speak, and he looked away from her as he said:

"What you have to do is to forget me. You will find, because you are so attractive, that men will come flocking to meet you. And since you can afford to entertain, you are sure to meet somebody sooner or later who will look after you and protect you as I am unable to do."

"Are you ... really suggesting that ... loving you as I do," Clova said, "I would be ... prepared to ... marry anybody ... else?"

"I cannot marry you!" Tarquil said quickly. "How can I? I can only ask you again to forget me."

He drew in his breath.

"I came to see you because you asked me to do so, and now I am going to say good-bye, Clova. It would be best if we do not see each other again until you at least are aware of how mistaken you are in your feelings towards me."

As he finished speaking, Clova made a sound like an animal that has been hurt. Then she asked:

"How can you be ... so cruel? How can you be so ... unkind? I shall never ... never love ...

anybody but you... and I cannot possibly cope with everything... I must do here... without you."

"That is what you have to do."

"Just because of my... money?" Clova asked. "If that is all that stands between us... then as far as I am concerned... I no longer... want it."

She felt as if Tarquil were hardly listening to her, and that if he was, he did not believe what she was saying.

Insistently she put out her hand to hold on to the lapels of his jacket.

"Listen to me," she said. "That money was not mine in the first place. It was given to my mother by a man who found her... attractive and amusing for a... short time until he remembered somewhat belatedly that he had a wife and children in South Africa."

She paused before she forced herself to continue.

"He was... paying for the... favours she had given him... making her, as Euan said, although I could... never think of it in that way, as nothing but a... harlot."

Tears came into Clova's eyes and ran down her cheeks as she went on.

"She never... enjoyed that... money, and if you feel it is... tainted and... unclean, then I will... send it to Jan Maskill's family in Johannesburg. I am sure they will be only too... willing to take back what their father... expended on a woman they would... despise."

The tears now blinded her eyes as she said brokenly:

"I was only... glad to have it because at the moment it came there was nothing... nothing... not even a few francs...between me and starvation. Now I can throw...myself on the...charity of the Clan...and if they will...have me...perhaps you will...find a place for me in your home."

It was impossible to say any more, and sobbing tempestuously, Clova moved to rest her head against Tarquil's shoulder.

His arms went round her, and as she cried so that her tears wetted the cloth jacket she heard him say wonderingly:

"Do you really love me as much as that?"

"I...love you so much that there is...nothing else in the...world but...you," Clova sobbed, "and...if you do not...want me...I wish I had been...brave enough last night to...throw myself from the tower...as I thought of doing."

His arms tightened.

"My ridiculous darling!" he said in a very different voice from the one he had used before. "You must not talk like that."

"It...is true," Clova insisted. "I...I cannot live without...you...whatever you may...feel about me."

She felt his lips on her forehead as he said:

"It is because I love you that I am trying to do what is right, and although it is hard, to behave like a gentleman."

"I do not...want you to be a...gentleman," Clova said. "I...I want you to be...my husband!"

She heard Tarquil give a short laugh before he said:

"My darling, my sweet! Is there anyone like you! I knew the moment I saw you that you were the woman I had been looking for all my life, who I thought must be merely a figment of my imagination, and could not possibly exist! Then suddenly you were there and I was complete, for you were the other half of myself."

"That is... what I feel... too," Clova whispered.

Now there was a faint light of hope in her eyes, and Tarquil thought as he looked down at her tear-stained cheeks and the softness of her lips that it was impossible for anyone to be more beautiful.

"I love you—God, how I love you!" he said. "But I know what you are asking me to do is wrong."

"It is right... absolutely right, as far as... we are concerned!" Clova insisted. "And I have told you ... if you hate... my money, we will send it back or... give it away."

"That is what we will do," Tarquil said quietly. "We will give it to those who need it, and if I can utilise it, as I should be able to do, your money will bring employment into the Highlands and it will be a blessing rather than a curse."

"That is what I... want it to be," Clova cried, "and, Tarquil, if I am really... as you say... the other part of you, then... everything that is... mine, including me, is yours. So how can you be so... foolish about it?"

"I told you I have my pride," Tarquil said, but he was smiling.

"And I have no pride," Clova answered. "So... please... Tarquil please, please I beg of you, if necessary on my knees, to marry me! I love you and I will do... anything you ask of me. I want to be... your wife, I want to be... with you... I want to work... with you, and have you... guard and protect me, and I am not too... proud to say... so."

Tarquil did not answer. He only kissed her demandingly, fiercely, possessively.

His kisses told her without words that although he loved her, he would always be her master, would always be the demanding, authoritative person in her life.

That was what she wanted.

She understood that unless she surrendered herself completely and absolutely to him, he would always feel that because of his relative poverty, he was imposing on her.

But there was only one thing that mattered, Clova thought as he kissed her and went on kissing her.

Nothing else in the whole world was important except that Tarquil should love her.

She would do anything, anything he asked of her, rather than lose him.

Although there might be difficulties ahead because of his pride, and because his Clan had not the standing of hers, she knew that somehow she would be tactful and clever enough to make him forget it.

"I love you! I love you... Tarquil!" she said aloud when he raised his head.

Her lips were a little bruised from his kisses, but now her eyes were shining and her cheeks were flushed.

"You are mine," he said fiercely, "mine! And no one shall take you from me! At the same time, my darling, I doubt if the McBlanes will approve of your choice of a husband."

"They did not worry about me in the past," Clova replied, "and if Uncle Rory had not died, I could have remained in exile without their giving me as much as... a thought!

"Now, since fate has brought me back to the Clan, I am prepared to devote my life to ... their services. At the same time ... I have no great idea of my ... importance."

She looked up at him, and there was a note of anxiety in her voice as she said:

"Y-you will not ... mind ... that Mama did not behave ... very well according to people like ... Euan McBlane and the Elders? I am afraid, too, that the Elders of the Kilcowans may disapprove of me, and think I am not the right ... wife for ... you."

"If they do, they will not say so to me," Tarquil replied.

Then with a faint smile he added:

"I realise, my darling, exactly what you are saying to me and why you are saying it, and I adore you for being so tactful."

He kissed her before he went on.

"But I know, as you do, that our love is greater than all the difficulties that we may both have to face personally."

"I do not want to ... think about ... them," Clova said quickly. "I just want to think about you ... and let you ... manage everything ... else."

"That is exactly what I intend to do," he replied.

He put his cheek very tenderly against hers as he said:

"You do not at all deceive me! Everything you say makes me realise how adorable you are and at the same time that when you want to have your own way, you are very clever about it."

Clova moved a little closer to him.

"I want my own way in only one thing," she whispered, "and that is that ... you should ... marry me."

He did not answer for a moment, and she looked at him a little apprehensively.

"I have been thinking it over," he said after a moment, "and I feel I should make up my own mind about you. So, my beautiful, fascinating little Chieftain, I will assert my prerogative as a man and ask you, if necessary of course on bended knee, if you will honour me by becoming my wife?"

Clova gave a little cry.

"You said it! That is what I ... wanted you to ... say! Oh, darling, darling Tarquil ... my answer is 'Yes!' I love you! I promise I will try in ... every way to make you ... happy."

Tarquil laughed.

"I will arrange that our wedding will be a demonstration to the whole of Scotland that the ancient hostility between the Clans is now out of date. In celebrating our marriage we will show this by making sure that a representative from every Clan in the Highlands is invited."

Clova clasped her hands together.

"Oh, Tarquil, what a wonderful idea! Nothing could be more effective, because I am sure everybody, wherever they live, all over the world, enjoys a wedding."

"And everybody loves a lover," Tarquil said quietly. "That is what we will be, my darling, lovers now and forever, setting an example of love and happiness to everybody we meet."

"Oh, Tarquil."

The tears were back in Clova's eyes, tears of happiness and joy as she knew he had surrendered to her insistence.

At the same time, he was showing the initiative and authority which would be his for the rest of their lives.

She put up her arm to draw his head down to hers.

"I love you... I love you!" she said. "There are no other... words in which I can... tell you how wonderful... you are!"

She saw the light in his eyes, and there was also a hint of fire in them.

Then he was kissing her once again, kissing her to show he not only adored and worshipped her, but also possessed her.

A Conqueror and a Victor after a hard battle.

ABOUT THE AUTHOR

Barbara Cartland, the world's most famous romantic novelist, who is also an historian, playwright, lecturer, political speaker and television personality, has now written over 430 books and sold over 400 million books the world over.

She has also had many historical works published and has written four autobiographies as well as the biographies of her mother and that of her brother, Ronald Cartland, who was the first Member of Parliament to be killed in the last war. This book has a preface by Sir Winston Churchill and has just been republished with an introduction by Sir Arthur Bryant.

Love at the Helm, a novel written with the help and inspiration of the late Admiral of the Fleet, the Earl Mountbatten of Burma, is being sold for the Mountbatten Memorial Trust.

Miss Cartland in 1978 sang an Album of Love Songs with the Royal Philharmonic Orchestra.

In 1976 by writing twenty-one books, she broke the world record and has continued for the following eight years with twenty-four, twenty, twenty-three, twenty-four, twenty-four, twenty-five, twenty-three, and twenty-six. She is in the *Guinness Book of Records* as the best-selling author in the world.

She is unique in that she was one and two in the Dalton List of Best Sellers, and one week had four books in the top twenty.

In private life Barbara Cartland, who is a Dame of the Order of St. John of Jerusalem, Chairman of the St. John Council in Hertfordshire and Deputy President of the St. John Ambulance Brigade, has also fought for better conditions and salaries for Midwives and Nurses.

Barbara Cartland is deeply interested in Vitamin Therapy and is President of the British National Association for Health. Her book *The Magic of Honey* has sold throughout the world and is translated into many languages. Her designs "Decorating with Love" are being sold all over the U.S.A., and the National Home Fashions League named her in 1981, "Woman of Achievement."

In 1984 she received at Kennedy Airport America's Bishop Wright Air Industry Award for her contribution to the development of aviation: in 1931 she and two R.A.F. Officers thought of, and carried, the first aeroplane-towed glider air-mail.

Barbara Cartland's Romances (a book of cartoons) has been published in Great Britain and the U.S.A., as well as a cookery book, *The Romance of Food*, and *Getting Older, Growing Younger*. She has recently written a children's pop-up picture book, entitled *Princess to the Rescue*.

BARBARA CARTLAND

Called after her own
beloved Camfield Place,
each Camfield novel of love
by Barbara Cartland
is a thrilling, never-before published
love story by the greatest romance
writer of all time.

May '87...AN ANGEL RUNS AWAY
June '87...FORCED TO MARRY
July '87...BEWILDERED IN BERLIN

More romance from
BARBARA CARTLAND

__08458-1	HELGA IN HIDING #30	$2.50
__08493-X	SAFE AT LAST #31	$2.75
__08512-X	HAUNTED #32	$2.75
__08568-5	CROWNED WITH LOVE #33	$2.75
__08579-0	ESCAPE #34	$2.75
__08606-1	THE DEVIL DEFEATED #35	$2.75
__08646-0	THE SECRET OF THE MOSQUE #36	$2.75
__08673-8	A DREAM IN SPAIN #37	$2.75
__08714-9	THE LOVE TRAP #38	$2.75
__08753-X	LISTEN TO LOVE #39	$2.75
__08795-5	THE GOLDEN CAGE #40	$2.75
__08837-4	LOVE CASTS OUT FEAR #41	$2.75
__08882-X	A WORLD OF LOVE #42	$2.75
__08906-0	DANCING ON A RAINBOW #43	$2.75
__08933-8	LOVE JOINS THE CLANS #44	$2.75

Available at your local bookstore or return this form to:

JOVE
THE BERKLEY PUBLISHING GROUP, Dept. B
390 Murray Hill Parkway, East Rutherford, NJ 07073

Please send me the titles checked above. I enclose _____. Include $1.00 for postage and handling if one book is ordered; add 25¢ per book for two or more not to exceed $1.75. CA, IL, NJ, NY, PA, and TN residents please add sales tax. Prices subject to change without notice and may be higher in Canada. Do not send cash.

NAME_____
ADDRESS_____
CITY_____ STATE/ZIP_____
(Allow six weeks for delivery.)